NURSE AT STE. MONIQUE

(Original title: *Stranger—Go Home!*)

by

JULIET ARMSTRONG

HARLEQUIN BOOKS
Winnipeg • Canada   New York • New York

NURSE AT STE. MONIQUE

First published in 1966 by Mills & Boon Limited,
50 Grafton Way, Fitzroy Square, London,
England, under the title *Stranger—Go Home!*

Harlequin edition published December, 1966

All the characters in this book have no existence outside the imagination of the Author, and have no relation whatsoever to anyone bearing the same name or names. They are not even distantly inspired by any individual known or unknown to the Author, and all the incidents are pure invention.

 The Harlequin trade mark, consisting of the word HARLEQUIN® and the portrayal of a Harlequin, is registered in the United States Patent Office and in the Canada Trade Marks Office.

Copyright, ©, 1966, by Juliet Armstrong. All rights reserved.

Printed in the U.S.A.

CHAPTER 1

IT was a foggy morning in November—a Monday morning at that—and Maura O'Shea, picking her way along Game Street, en route for St. Matthew's Hospital, felt thoroughly irritable and depressed.

Her third winter in London, and if this was a sample of what to expect it would be her worst.

It was partly her own fault, of course, for choosing to live out instead of staying on comfortably in the Nurses' Home. But it had sounded such fun, sharing a flat with Gwen in one of those early Victorian terraces in Islington. She hadn't realised, and Gwen hadn't warned her, how horrible it could be, leaping out of a warm bed, pulling on uniform grown suddenly and maliciously intractable, and plunging into a dark, cold street before the near-by church clock struck half past seven.

"I can't imagine anything more revolting," she muttered to herself, cautiously increasing her pace as the lights of Game Street Underground glimmered through the mist.

But the next moment made nonsense of her grumble.

Someone stole up behind her, dealt her a violent blow on the back of her arm and snatching her handbag, disappeared.

Too near the edge of the kerb, she lost her balance and crashed into the gutter, crying out furiously as she picked herself up: "Stop thief! He's got my handbag!"

Passers-by began to collect, and a tall man, carrying a suitcase, strode over to her and lifted her to her feet with his free arm, firmly but gently, as though she were a precious piece of china.

"It's a damned disgrace," he said indignantly, his arm still round her, steadying her. "A nurse, of all people! Are you badly hurt?"

"No, I'm not. It's my handbag I'm worried about," she exclaimed breathlessly. "Can't anyone stop him?"

"My brother went after him. And look! He's got your bag—and the brute who grabbed it. Here, keep guard over my suitcase for a minute while I help hold the swine."

He went off, returning a moment or two later, hatless and grasping a wildly struggling and most unprepossessing individual by one arm, while another rather younger man, his brother no doubt, hung on to the other.

"Lemme go! You got the perishin' bag, ain't you?" the thief was shouting. And when some of the bystanders called out uncomplimentary remarks about the sort of people who robbed poor young nurses of their hard-earned wages, he retorted indignantly that he couldn't see it was a something nurse in the something fog, and made fresh and even more frantic efforts to break free.

But the men holding him tightened their grip, and before anyone could obey the stentorian demand of one of them to fetch a policeman, a constable appeared to enquire sternly what this "carry-on" meant.

His appearance had anything but a calming effect on the captive, who reiterated clamorously that as the lady had got her lousy bag back he ought to be allowed to go instead of being rough-handled and probably injured for life by "these perishers."

Maura, dishevelled and hating to be stared at, and desiring most earnestly to get to work, was in hearty agreement with this. Goodness knew how long she would be delayed if this very competent-looking constable took an official view of the matter.

It was soon clear that this was just what he was doing.

With the man who had first seized the thief assisting him, he led the way to the nearest police station, Maura, and the man with the suitcase, obeying his polite but firm request to follow him.

Maura soon discovered that her companion was suffering even greater inconvenience.

He and his brother, she learned on that short, embarrassing walk, were visitors to London, and staying at Game Street Station Hotel. They had just emerged, meaning to go by Underground to Euston. They were to breakfast there—quickly—and then he was to catch a train for the North, where he had business matters to attend to.

She looked up at him in dismay, noticing then for the first time that he was distinguished-looking rather than handsome, with bronzed complexion and steady grey eyes.

"Does missing your train mean that you'll also be behindhand with important engagements?" she asked in distress.

"I'll probably fix to go by air. We do most of our travelling by plane, where we come from—the Caribbean. Anyway," and he smiled reassuringly, "there's nothing for you to worry about so far as I'm concerned. You're the one who deserves all the sympathy. You must be shocked, as well as badly bruised."

"You didn't get off so very easily," she declared ruefully. "I wonder your arm wasn't wrenched out of its socket. Even that hefty policeman's got his work cut out. As for your poor brother——"

"Oh, Claude will think it a lark—in retrospect, anyway. He'll be dining out on the story of this adventure for weeks when we're back home."

"And you yourself won't be talking about it at all?" Despite her pain and discomfort she was faintly amused at his Big Brother tone.

"You bet I will." He was smiling down at her again. "But my account won't be quite so dramatic. I'm older and duller than my brother—and not such a social success!"

They had reached the police-station now, and while her assailant, still fighting and yelling, was taken off—presumably to the charge room—she and the brothers were escorted to an upstairs office where an Inspector prepared to take their statements.

Maura who, like most nurses, had always found the police helpful and friendly, felt no nervousness as she gave her brief version of the incident. And the two men, having made their statements, too, remarked with evident relief that if this was all that was required of them, they certainly hadn't been held up too long.

But a shock was in store for all of them.

The Inspector informed them, pleasantly but decisively, that they would be asked to attend the Cloth Hall Magistrate's Court in due course, reasonable notice being given them. Meanwhile the man in custody would be taken with the least possible delay before the magistrate for a preliminary hearing.

Then, while the brothers looked at him in dismay, he added: "And that may not be the end of it, I'm afraid. You may be required to repeat your evidence at another court."

"But we're not resident here," the elder one exclaimed. "Our stay here is limited."

The Inspector nodded.

"That will be conveyed to the proper quarters," he said. "But you must remember, Mr. Lasalle, that robbery with violence is a very serious charge."

Paul—the brother who had just spoken—glanced at the clock on the wall.

"I suggest, Miss O'Shea, that you come to our hotel and have breakfast with us," he said. "Or coffee, anyway. You look rather shaken."

"An excellent idea, if I may say so," the Inspector put in, bestowing a fatherly smile on Maura. "But you'll want to telephone the hospital. I'll get the number for you if you like."

A few moments later Maura was explaining to the Sister in charge of D Ward the reason for her failure to arrive on time, and asking permission to get a quick cup of coffee before coming along.

"Very well. I'll expect you shortly. Glad you got your bag back, anyway." And with that practical observation Sister Foster rang off.

The Game Street Station Hotel was old-fashioned, not to say dowdy. But it was quiet and spacious, and after a hurried wash and tidy up, which included sticking some plaster on her grazed knees, Maura felt less dismal—her most immediate distress being the knowledge that her stockings were ruined.

Excellent coffee and rolls, in company with delightful hosts, took her mind, however, off holes and ladders and bruises. To her surprise she found that she was positively enjoying herself.

Paul and Claude Lasalle, she learned, had family

plantations in the West Indies. Citrus fruits were their main interest, but they also exported cocoa beans and spices.

"It sounds very romantic," Maura commented, her long-lashed blue eyes dreamy. "Now, my life is just plain ordinary. I'm a run-of-the-mill Irish girl, nursing in London."

"Personally I think that nursing is one of the finest jobs in the world." There was the ring of sincerity in Paul's deep voice. And Claude remarked, with his attractively boyish smile, that she must be strangely lacking in vanity if she could apply such an absurd label to herself as "run-of-the-mill."

She disregarded the compliment and said frankly: "I'm not fully trained yet, and none too sure of passing my finals next summer." Adding disconsolately: "It won't help me to get into scrapes of this sort—having to hang about the courts repeating evidence about a matter I'd far sooner put out of my mind. Missing lectures, and all that."

And then she looked at her watch.

"I must go. We'll be meeting again—pretty soon, let's hope—at Cloth Hall Court."

And with a quick good-bye to both of them, and a thank-you for their hospitality, she fairly ran on her way—the cup of coffee having taken a little longer than Sister might think reasonable.

However Sister, in her terse way, proved surprisingly sympathetic.

"I'd send you off duty if I could spare you," she said, "but you know how things are in D Ward just now. I'll get you some fresh stockings—and then you must just carry on, I'm afraid."

Crossing the hospital yard that evening on her

way to the bus stop for Islington, Maura groaned when she suddenly caught sight of Claude Lasalle waiting for her. She was feeling exhausted. All she wanted was to get home and curl up in bed with a hot bottle, not make herself pleasant to any young man. Though if it had been the elder brother—Paul—!

"Please don't think this frightful nerve of me." Claude seemed to sense that he was unwelcome. "I wanted to know if you were all right."

"How did you find out what time I'd come off duty?" she demanded, trying not to speak stiffly.

"Oh, a porter was sympathetic. Mind you, I didn't mention any names. But listen! Paul caught a later train to the North, and I'm all alone. Won't you take pity on me, and have dinner with me? I'm—I'm no wolf, truly."

She hesitated. Gwen Davies, the friend she lived with—doing night duty at present—had said she would be out from four o'clock onwards. It would be distinctly depressing getting supper for herself in an empty flat.

"So long as I get home early," she said. "And please don't take me anywhere grand. Somewhere simple and quiet, please. I'm very tired."

His face cleared.

"I've discovered a little place in Piccadilly where they have West Indian food, and where the coffee is nearly as good as at home. Better than what we had this morning, and that's saying something. Our coffee is famous, you know."

"Indeed I do." She smiled at him. "The friend I share a flat with has relatives in Raballo. They send her a sealed tin every Christmas."

"Well, come and try the Pink Pelican. Here's the

bus." And off they went, not, as Sister Foster had advised, straight home to Islington, but in the direction of Piccadilly Circus.

It was Claude who did most of the talking as they sat at dinner in the Pink Pelican, and soon his friendliness, and his frank admiration, together with the excellent food and drink, made her relax. She listened, with growing interest, to his description of the islands in the Caribbean where the Lasalle family had for centuries owned estates.

He spoke well, conjuring up pictures of mile-long, sunlit bays, fringed with coconut palms where, all the year round, one could bathe in the warm blue sea and picnic on golden sands: took her, in imagination, driving with him on switchback roads through the mountains, looking down on valleys over which was flung a mantle of green forest, splashed here and there with the sudden brilliant colours of tall flowering trees—yellow and pink, mauve and scarlet—and the flash of bright birds.

But it wasn't all Paradise, he assured her, his tone becoming sober. There was plenty of hard work to be done in the Caribbean, with the surge towards industrialisation as a means of providing a better livelihood for the teeming population.

Indeed it was with the object of searching for the most satisfactory modern machinery for processing citrus fruits that he and his brother had come to England, both having undergone training in engineering as well as in tropical agriculture.

"We want capital, of course, in the islands," he went on, "but we're getting that. And the tourists are coming, now that the Americans are putting up fine hotels and that ships are being built here, there and everywhere, for West Indian cruising. But we need folk with skills who'll settle down to training some of our less educated. We even," and he smiled, "need nurses to replace those we keep sending over here."

Her eyes shone at that.

"That's something Gwen would like to hear," she exclaimed. "She's always talking about Raballo—how thrilling it would be to go and stay out there with her cousins—taking a temporary job at a hospital."

"What's stopping her?" Claude demanded, quirking an eyebrow.

"Like me, she hasn't taken her finals yet," Maura told him. "And it would be a step in the dark for her." Adding impulsively: "You must come to the flat some time, and talk to her about things."

She hadn't really meant to invite him, and half regretted it. People were always warning one about the dangers of encouraging strange young men.

But he looked far from sinister as, his bronzed face boyishly eager, his grey eyes smiling, he observed quickly that he'd love to accept her invitation.

"Paul and I know hardly anyone of our own age in England," he said. "We're still in our twenties—I'm twenty-six and he's twenty-eight—and our business is nearly all with deadly solemn business men and their stout, pompous wives."

She laughed at that.

"Haven't they offspring for you to play around with?"

He gave a resentful grunt.

"Long-haired teenagers who look on us, in turn, as has-beens! No! I can tell you, Maura, now Paul's away I'm going to be damned lonely."

"I suppose we're less sociable over here than in the West Indies?"

"I should say so. People are so cold and stiff—and in such a hurry."

The note of homesickness in his voice struck an immediate chord in her.

She was happy in London now, she said, but when she had first left Galway and come to train at St. Matthew's Hospital she had felt utterly forlorn. Indeed she had been desperately tempted, more than once, to pack up and run home to Ireland—to the little town where everyone knew her and called her by her Christian name.

"Your family must have missed you terribly," he said, his eyes resting on her pensive face—so like a frangipani blossom from the tree in the garden of his mother's home, he thought, with its delicate colouring.

"Not all that much," she told him thoughtfully. "I'm the youngest, and only single one of the family, and my parents are long dead. I'm very fond of my brothers and sisters, and they of me, but they're all married, with children coming along." She paused. "Nothing's the same when your parents have gone."

He nodded understandingly.

"I'm lucky. I still have my mother, and she's a darling. Paul, too, of course. Though actually he's my half-brother. He was a small baby when his mother, my father's first wife, died. But I think he loves my mother as much as I do. Certainly"—his voice was rueful now, his eyes downcast, "he doesn't give her half the trouble that I do."

"What sort of trouble do you give her?" she asked, not taking him very seriously.

He shrugged his shoulders.

"I'm far more selfish. People find him hard and arrogant sometimes—people he doesn't approve of!

But he's a wonderful chap, really. I wish I could live up to him."

"And are you the only two?"

"Unfortunately. I'd have loved to have a sister."

"And neither of you is married?"

He seemed surprised at the directness of her question, and she was immediately ashamed of her gaucheness. Would she never acquire a touch, at least, of sophistication? Would she always remain an outspoken country girl from the back of beyond?

And then he shook his head sombrely.

"No," he said, "we're neither of us married." And his tone made her feel clumsier than ever—implying, almost that there had been an ill-starred romance for one of them—a broken engagement, perhaps.

She was not one to force a confidence and she was relieved when, with a sudden change of mood, he announced that, sad as he was to lose her company, he thought it was high time she went home and had a rest.

"I'll drop you at your flat and then make tracks for Victoria Station. I've booked in at a smaller hotel there than the one in Game Street." He sounded brisk and businesslike now. "I'll give you my card with the address and telephone number, and hope you'll be a dear and ring me. I'd be bitterly disappointed not to see you again until we meet in court."

She appreciated his leaving the initiative to her. He was clearly not the pushing sort—as she had been half afraid when she had found him waiting for her outside the hospital.

She would ring him up some day soon when Gwen was free to help entertain him. They would rake up another man to make a fourth, and perhaps manage a little supper party—something easy that didn't keep one sticking around the kitchen.

Though it would be fun to achieve the surprise of a real West Indian dish—a *pilau* of chicken and rice, perhaps.

True to his word, Claude neither wrote nor telephoned to Maura.

Two days after their first encounter, however, a district messenger arrived at the Islington flat with a spray of huge brilliant red flowers which Gwen, who happened to open the front door, declared with conviction were poinsettias.

"And fresh, not artificial," she commented admiringly. "They must have cost this new boy-friend of yours a packet—flown from the West Indies to some posh Mayfair florist!"

"He's not my boy-friend," Maura protested, hunting for a vase large enough to accommodate the flowers. "As I've told you, I think his elder brother is even more attractive. There's something special about him. I can't quite explain."

"Forget Paul, or whatever his name is, and concentrate on the one who's around," Gwen advised sagely. "You'll have to ring him up now and thank him. And what about suggesting a day for this famous supper party? It will have to be a Saturday. It's the only time we'll both be here."

"We'll need another man," Maura pondered aloud. "Alec Rogers, from Casualty, seems to want to be friendly—"

Gwen's brown eyes twinkled.

"Leave that to me, my dear. We don't want one of your hangers-on. A lot of fun we'd have with the pair of them glaring at each other."

"O.K., ask who you like, Gwen. But it's a terrible pity it can't be Paul Lasalle. It's not only that he's big and kind—"

"But, by your own account, you've hardly spoken to him." Gwen was growing impatient. "Surely you don't want both these brothers running after you—to say nothing of Alec Rogers and a few more."

She expected Maura to flare up at that, but she didn't. She merely remarked absently: "It's not like that at all, Gwen. You know that quite well. But he was so strong and so gentle, the way he picked me up after that wretch had sent me flying into the gutter."

A remark which Gwen, who at twenty-three was a year older than Maura, and far older in sophistication, greeted with a tolerant, "Well, well, well!"

The party was a great success. Gwen's friend, one George Smith, was an amateur pop singer as well as a student in his last year at St. Matthew's Hospital, and when he found that Claude could produce from his memory a string of calypsos, he took to him at once, and twanged them out on his guitar, the girls joining in the chorus.

He had a most attractive tenor voice, had Claude, and a most infectious laugh, and by the end of the evening Maura was well on the way to forgetting any imagined preference for Paul.

Gwen, she found, shared her enthusiasm, and they decided as, their guests having departed, they prepared for bed, that Claude was one of the best-mannered and most thoughtful men they had ever met. Quite unconscious of his good looks, he seemed, and though he was doubtless accustomed to being waited on hand and foot when at home in the Caribbean, he was not only ready to help clear away the supper things but insisted on washing them up—with remarkable speed and efficiency.

"George is cleverer, of course," Gwen maintained loyally. "Look what he made of those calypsos after Claude had given him the idea. But Claude's a jolly nice chap, and the only pity is that he'll be off in no time to the West Indies." She sighed. "It's always the way with the men one feels one could fall for. Either they live abroad—or else they're married—"

"Neither of the Lasalles is married," Maura told her.

Gwen pulled her nightdress over her brown hair; she looked at her sharply.

"How do you know?" she demanded.

"I asked!" Maura admitted, feeling rather uncomfortable.

"Well, I'm blowed." Gwen went into a peal of laughter. "You're not losing any time. I wonder you didn't frighten him off."

This time Maura's Irish temper did send out a spark.

"Personally I don't share you English girls' obsession with marriage," she said loftily. "But I just don't care to go around with someone who's got a wife and children parked away."

"Excellent sentiments, darling," Gwen teased. "You continue to concentrate on your lectures—and pleasing Sister Foster. Though if, to use your own phrase, you're intending to go around with this chap, you won't find good resolutions too easy to keep. I bet he'll try to monopolise all your spare time."

Maura grunted.

"I'm not a fool," she said.

Her friendship with Claude certainly made swift headway, and she found that Gwen was right in one respect. Considerate as he seemed in many ways, he simply could not realise how hard she worked; how important she felt it to give full attention to lectures, to turn up for duty reasonably fresh and alert.

"It will do you good to come out and dance—and shake off the hospital atmosphere," was his plea, and he looked as disappointed as a child when she had to insist on a reasonable number of early nights.

She had difficulty, too, in persuading him to take her to modestly priced restaurants and clubs. She realised that he wanted to give her the best, but it embarrassed her to see him peeling off pound notes as though he were a millionaire. Then, too, she had only two evening dresses, neither in the height of fashion. And though he declared that wherever he took her she outshone every other woman, she knew that this was sheer nonsense.

Of course it was a touching kind of nonsense. And so was his gratitude to her for going out with him.

"You're an angel of kindness," he assured her, adding on one occasion: "You make me forget all my troubles."

They were dancing at a club in Soho, when he told her that, and she looked up at him with concern.

"Have you so many troubles, Claude?" she asked him. "I should have thought you had most of the good things of life. Youth, health, interesting and worthwhile work in a glorious climate—what can you have to make you depressed?"

He shrugged his shoulders.

"Business negotiations can be terribly harassing," he said, after an almost imperceptible pause. "I haven't the temperament for them. In fact, if it wasn't for you, I'd feel like leaving everything to Paul, who's much tougher, and going home. As it is," and he held her very close to him for a moment, "Ste. Monique has lost all its charms for me. I shall find it almost unbearable, saying good-bye to you."

"I shall miss you, too," she said; and though she intended to sound poised and sensible, there was a hint of wistfulness in her voice. "You've been very sweet to me, very kind."

"Have I, darling? I wonder!"

He was looking down at her with an expression she could not fathom.

"You've certainly been different from many of the boys who've taken me out," she told him candidly. "I've been at ease with you. Not on my guard, in case you started getting fresh!"

"That's because you are you, Maura. Not ignorant! How could you be? But you have a touching sort of innocence." And then he gave a broad smile. "All the same, you could deal out a very smart box on the ear, if you thought a chap deserved it."

She smiled back at him.

"I could that," she said equably. "I've a temper, like all my clan. No angels among us."

Several times she went out with him—to dances, to the ballet and, when she protested that an early night was a necessity to her, to dinner at one or other modest restaurant not too far from home.

After three weeks the summons came to appear at Cloth Hall Court—and with it the prospect of renewing her acquaintance with Paul. For whether he wished to or not he would have to come South to give evidence against the man who had snatched her bag in Game Street.

She had thought less and less about him as time had gone by, and wondered whether that first strange attraction she had felt for him would show any sign of revival. Three weeks was not a very long time, but Claude's lively society, and his—his sweetness—you couldn't call it anything else—had blurred Paul's image. She couldn't remember what it was about him that had made him seem so special, or why she had thought him more attractive than Claude. He had had an air of distinction, certainly, which Claude could not claim. But not Claude's regular good looks.

Claude had insisted on fetching her to the court in a taxi, and there they found Paul waiting for them. At first he seemed as sympathetic and cordial as ever and she warmed to him again, remembering his gentleness, his concern for her.

But when the case in which they were involved came on, and they were sent out of the court, into a deserted passage, while the constable gave evidence, things became slightly strained.

"Sit down here, darling," Claude said, guiding Maura to a bench by the wall. "And let me turn your coat collar down, or you'll feel it when we go out into the fresh air again."

At that Paul eyed them both with surprise.

"You two have evidently been getting to know each other," he said coolly. "Odd of you not to mention it, Claude, when you wrote. I asked you if you had seen anything more of Miss O'Shea."

Claude looked disconcerted. "Didn't I tell you?" he returned with a not too successful attempt at sounding casual. "I certainly meant to. Maura has been very kind, taking pity on my solitary state."

Paul gave him a considering glance, but said nothing, and Claude tried quickly to change the subject with a comment on English court procedure.

Maura, sorry for his embarrassment, made a light rejoinder, but she was greatly puzzled. Why did Paul object to a friendship between herself and his brother? Surely he couldn't be jealous, when he had made no move whatever to keep in touch with her himself Staying in the North wouldn't make it impossible to send flowers. There was always Interflora. Or he could have written a line to ask her how she was faring.

It was a relief when they were called back, one by one, to give evidence, and when they were sitting together in the court, listening to the testimony of the doctor from Brixton Prison, the tension between them lessened. Their interest was held by the case and, in particular, by the changed appearance of the defendant. He seemed dull and vacant—shrunken, almost —and quite incapable of anything approaching violence.

Hearing from the doctor supporting evidence that the accused had undoubtedly taken a large dose of so-called purple hearts the evening before the attack, they hoped now that the case would end with a fine and a warning.

But no! As the constable had told them before, the man—drug addict or not—had committed the serious offence of robbery with violence. Even had anyone come forward to offer bail it would not have been accepted. Back to Brixton he had to go, there to wait until the case came on at the Central Criminal Court.

Paul was particularly disappointed. His presence was urgently needed in the Caribbean, and here he was, stuck for an indefinite period in Europe, when he was just about to finish his business here.

"Let's take Maura out to lunch and talk things over," Claude suggested, as they walked out into the street.

"I'm afraid I can't. I have barely time to snatch a sandwich and get my plane to Scotland," Paul returned quickly. "We've our final discussion this evening. After that I shall be paying a brief visit to Turin, then probably flying home."

"But what about this case?" Claude demanded. "You said just now—"

"I've done some rapid thinking while we've been walking down this street," Paul said shortly. "I shall fly back when they send for me. It's a ridiculous waste of money, but not so expensive, probably, as hanging about in Europe."

They stopped then at the corner, waiting for a taxi, and he looked at Claude.

"What about you? How are things going?"

"I'm not through yet with Ballon Brothers," Claude told him. "I shall stay here for the moment, and try to make them reduce their estimate."

"I see." Paul's voice was dry. "Well, as I seem more in a hurry than you two, I'll take this taxi, if you don't mind. Good-bye, Miss O'Shea."

But Maura's temper was flaring at what she considered Paul's rudeness. A bus came along just before the taxi drew up, and with the briefest, " 'Bye," which included both men, she jumped in and was whisked off in the direction of the hospital.

How could she possibly have thought herself attracted to Paul? she wondered, her face flushed with indignation. She had imagined him kindly and courteous, a gentleman to his finger-tips—and here he was behaving like a boor.

Why should it annoy him that she and Claude had become friendly, these last three weeks? What business was it of his? Was it that he suspected her of setting her cap at Claude, and regarded her as on a lower social level than the Lasalles?

She recalled with disgust the comments he had made on nursing as a profession, over that hurried breakfast at Game Street Station Hotel. What humbug!

And Claude—she wasn't altogether pleased with him, either. Was he scared of this elder brother of his? Wouldn't it have been fairer to her to let Paul know beforehand of their growing friendship—instead of dropping "darlings" all over the place?

It was good to be back at the hospital and on duty, after a snack in the canteen. The patients in D Ward—medical cases of varying seriousness—liked her. She couldn't help knowing it. And she, for her part, though a child in age compared with most of them, had an almost motherly feeling towards them. It was their dependence on her for so much of their comfort, of course—their instinct that no trouble was too much for her—their knowledge that even if they were fractious she would understand that few people in pain were invariably reasonable.

"This is my real life—nursing," she told herself, as she settled the women down for their afternoon rest. "I'll be a fool if I take these Lasalles too seriously. In a few weeks they'll be back in the West Indies, right out of my ken. What will it matter then that Claude is attractive, and Paul a mannerless oaf? Before long I shall have forgotten what either of them looked like—and a jolly good thing, too."

But those brave sentiments took a shaky turn that very same evening.

She had barely finished her solitary supper—Gwen having left early for St. Matthew's—when there was a knock at the front door, and there stood Claude with a large bunch of freesias, their perfume spilling into the air.

"I'm sorry, Claude, but you've chosen a bad evening," she said, not inviting him in. "I'm very tired, and I'm set for a hot bath and an early night."

"Darling, you must let me in for five minutes—if it's only to apologise for Paul's appalling rudeness to you," he pleaded.

She hesitated, then with a little shrug of her shoulders, she took the freesias from him, and let him in.

"Paul would be still more angry if he realised what a lot of money you spend on me," she said, as she shut the door. "These freesias—goodness knows what they must have cost you."

"Nothing's half good enough for you, Maura." He drew her into his arms, flowers and all, and kissed her on the lips.

She let him hold her for a minute or two, laying her dark head on his shoulder.

"I ought to be thoroughly annoyed with you—as well as with Paul," she said. "But I'm just tired and dispirited. Why didn't you tell Paul we'd been going around together, ever since that morning I had my bag snatched?"

"Why should I?" he countered. "It's no business of his. He's far too interfering, is Paul—always finding fault with me over something, just because he's older and has a more important position in the firm."

She broke away from him.

"Why don't you stand up to him?"

"Because in so many ways he's a damned good chap—a much more estimable character than I am."

"I find that hard to believe," was her curt comment. "Anyway, Claude, it's much better if we stop seeing each other. After all, within a month or two, when the case at the Old Bailey is over, you'll be back in the Caribbean—and we aren't likely to see each other again."

"Why do you say that, Maura?"

"Because it's the way things happen. For a year or two we might exchange cards at Christmas—even, possibly, at birthdays. But then, by degrees, we'd forget—and that would be that."

"I could never forget you, Maura. You're so sweet, so lovely!"

"Never is a long time! But about Paul—doesn't he know that calling people 'darling' doesn't mean a thing? In England, anyway—!"

"We're old-fashioned, in some respects, out in the West Indies. Victorian! But"—he hesitated—"I don't think Paul was shocked on that score. He probably realised by the tone of my voice that I'd grown very fond of you."

"And he thinks I'm not good enough to be a friend of yours."

He gave a short laugh.

"More likely sees it the other way round. That, as a human being, I'm your inferior—in most ways at least."

"Well, I'm not really interested." She pretended to smother a little yawn. "It's been fun going about with you. But I don't want to fall down on my work. Sister asked me the other day if I was getting enough sleep—and reminded me that it's not so very long before I take my Finals."

"O.K., we'll cut it down to twice a week." He took her hands and kissed them. "Please, darling, don't banish me altogether. I'd be utterly miserable, here in London, but isolated from you." And then, very gently, he tilted up her chin and looked down into her eyes. "You'd miss me, too—just a little. Why should we make ourselves unhappy before there's any need?"

She tried to be firm with him, realising painfully that for all he said about his affection for her, about never forgetting her, he visualised no shared future for them.

"I must train myself to think that way, too," she told herself, ashamed of her susceptibility to his charm. "To live for the day." And she said, serenely and with a smile: "Very well—twice a week. And now please go, Claude dear. I'm tired. I want to be alone."

Claude's acquiescence over spending only two evenings a week with her should have relieved her. She had been afraid that when it came to the point he would try to wrangle with her over it.

But things didn't work out the way she had intended.

Instead of cooling off, his protestations of affection became more and more ardent, and his kisses more passionate, so that she had to force herself to pull him up, to show him decisively that she drew a hard and fast line where lovemaking was concerned. It wasn't easy, for each time they met the attraction she felt for him increased. But her upbringing stood her in good stead—that, and his failure to breathe a word about a possible marriage between them, even in the remote future.

In a matter of weeks there came the summons to go to the Central Criminal Court, and once again she and Paul and Claude—Paul having flown back from the Caribbean—attended a court of justice.

There was a greater air of solemnity here than at the Cloth Hall. Judge and barristers were bewigged, and the majesty of the law seemed a telling phrase. A cough or sneeze would have been as out of place as in a Quaker meeting.

Once more the Lasalles and Maura were sent out, and then called back separately to give evidence, but this time their waiting was among other people, which meant less awkwardness—for Maura, at least. They could not, even had they wished, have carried on a private conversation.

At last, back in court, sitting together on a hard bench, they heard the verdict on the man who had snatched Maura's bag, all those weeks ago.

He was sent not to prison, but to hospital, there to be treated for drug addiction.

Again the three of them left the court together, and this time Paul seemed in a gentler mood. On this occasion it was Claude who had to leave quickly, to keep a business appointment, and to Maura's amazement Paul asked her quietly if she would give him the pleasure of lunching with him.

Involuntarily her eyes went to Claude who, almost imperceptibly, shook his head, and at once she made an excuse for refusing Paul's invitation.

She told herself that she would have refused it anyway, but in her heart of hearts she wasn't too sure. He might have wished to apologise to her for his previous rudeness.

As it was, he echoed her polite regrets, and they parted, each going their separate ways.

That evening Claude was waiting for her when she left the hospital, and told her, looking very depressed indeed, that he and Paul would be returning by air to the West Indies in two days' time. This would, indeed, be his very last chance of seeing her, for he and

Paul had to "tie up things" together in London before leaving.

Maura's heart sank. She had tried to take a sensible view of their inevitable parting, but now it came to the point she knew that she was going to miss Claude terribly.

"How shall we spend our last evening, darling?" he was murmuring, slipping his hand through her arm. "Would you like to go to a show, or just dine quietly with me somewhere?"

For a moment Maura was silent. Then she said steadily: "Don't think me unkind—unappreciative—Claude! But I'd rather say good-bye here and now. In fact, my mind's made up to do just that."

He pleaded, walking with her towards her bus stop, for she would not let him take her home in a taxi: argued, even stormed. But she was adamant. She made her solitary way home to the empty Islington flat, and once there, collapsed on her bed in a flood of tears.

She was a fool—all kinds of a fool—to care so much that Claude was going away—that she would, in all probability, never see him again. Hadn't she, from the beginning of their friendship, known instinctively that it would end just this way?

Apart from the fatigue of hanging about the court, and her distress over Claude, the time she had spent on duty had been one rush, and presently she dropped off into a troubled sleep.

Around midnight she awoke to find that, unhappy or not, she was extremely hungry, and having made herself tea and scrambled eggs, she undressed and went back to bed.

Next morning she awoke, weary no longer, but sunk in depression, and was thankful to get to work, and to assure Sister Foster that she had finished with courts of law—for ever and ever, she hoped.

"So do I, Nurse!" Sister's tone was frosty, but Maura did not resent it. This wretched business of her handbag had laid a heavy load on Sister and on the young student nurse who had been trying so valiantly to make herself useful. To be amiable over it would have been difficult, even for a canonised saint.

She soon found herself far too busy to fret. There was the usual routine of bed-making and tidying up for the doctors' rounds, taking temperatures, measuring out medicine, giving injections and attending lectures—many of which activities entailed a considerable amount of clerical work.

And back at the little flat in Islington, there was housework to do, her "smalls" to wash, and a dash to the shops for groceries and vegetables.

Her mind was set on an early supper and bed, but on her return from her shopping expedition she had a shock. Pacing along the road outside the flat was Claude.

She stopped short, hardly knowing whether she was deliriously joyful, indignant, or despairingly sorrowful. And as he strode up to her, she demanded in a low, shaky voice: "Oh, Claude—why have you come?"

"To ask you to marry me, Maura," he returned desperately. "I found I couldn't go away without speaking to you. I realised it as soon as I left you. I've been feeling quite frantic."

For a moment it seemed to Maura that the pavement was tilting up in the strangest fashion. Then it righted itself, and she exclaimed, taking in Claude's haggard appearance: "You look terrible. As though you hardly know what you're saying. But come in, anyway, and sit down."

"I feel ghastly," he told her in a strangled tone, as he followed her into the house. "I was walking up and down this road half the night. And when I saw your light go on round about midnight, and then a light go on in the kitchen, I nearly came up and knocked on your door."

"I'm glad you didn't," she said, forcing herself to speak lightly. "That would definitely have set the neighbours talking."

"I know. Once I guessed from the dark windows that you had settled down, I went back to the hotel, and tried to sleep, myself."

They were in the flat now, and she switched on the sitting-room light. Her heart was beating unnaturally fast: she knew that the next moment she would be in his arms, that he would be showering kisses on her.

But the first thing he did was to pull a tiny velvet case from his pocket, spring it open, and show her a sapphire and diamond ring.

"I bought this for you this morning," he said in an oddly humble voice. "I want you to wear it—and come out to Ste. Monique to marry me, as soon as you've finished your training. Will you—my darling?"

She looked at him, a deep question in her eyes.

"If you've been wanting to marry me, why all this good-bye for ever business? Why all this suffering—for both of us?"

His face lit up then. "If you've been unhappy too, that means you *are* going to marry me." And now he made to slip the ring on her finger.

But she drew her hand away, still uncertain, and

reminded him quietly: "You still haven't answered my question."

He was silent for a full minute, looking down at her. Then he said: "Shall we say because I'm thoroughly selfish, and enjoyed being a free-as-air bachelor? But that now I simply cannot endure to live without you?"

Before she could answer he had made a second successful effort to put the ring on her engagement finger, and was sweeping her into his arms, kissing her lips, her eyes, her throat and telling her over and over again, half pleading, half exultant, that he loved her with all his heart, and always would.

"I love you, too, Claude." She could not keep back the little cry—could not resist his kisses.

At last, when he set her free, she said, her eyes suddenly filling with tears:

"Is love enough? How can I marry you and live out there if your family disapprove? Paul, for one, would be my bitter enemy. I feel that strongly."

He shook his head.

"Maybe Paul thinks I'm not responsible enough for marriage. I've sowed some pretty flourishing wild oats, you know. You'll have to forgive me, Maura—and believe that with you as my wife I'll never want to look at another woman. For it's the truth—I'm ready to swear it."

"You're honest with me—that's what counts, Claude," she said slowly. "Please God, we'll make a go of it. And now," her voice changed, and she smiled, "I'm going to cook us some supper, and send you off—with an *au revoir*, not a good-bye. We'll write a lot, and the time will soon pass."

"It will drag," Claude told her disconsolately.

"Still," and his expression lightened, "I'll be busy getting our home ready."

"That's fine." Her heart was singing now. "Come along with you, and peel some potatoes."

Gwen came in just as they were finishing supper. Off duty for forty-eight hours, she had been spending the day with relations and now looked forward to a peaceful evening watching the television.

But the sight of the sapphire ring on Maura's finger banished all such notions. This was clearly an occasion for celebration. She rummaged in the sideboard for a precious bottle of cherry brandy, and made a good strong brew from her last tin of Raballo coffee. And though the cups and glasses were odd sizes and shapes, and there wasn't quite so much cherry brandy left in the bottle as she had imagined, Maura's heart warmed towards her friend. She was a real sport, was Gwen.

When Claude had gone, however, with a lingering good-bye to Maura in the little hall, Gwen seemed less enthusiastic.

As she and Maura cleared away and washed up, she was singularly silent, asking at last, hesitatingly: "Are you sure, Maura, it's wise to get engaged to someone you know so little? He's a nice chap—but living so far away—!"

She was annoyed with herself at once for her tactlessness. Why hadn't she left things alone until tomorrow? She was always putting her great foot into it.

But to her surprise and relief Maura neither burst into tears nor rushed into a heated defence of her actions.

She pointed out reasonably that there was no question of a hasty marriage. She had every intention of sitting for her finals in June, and probably wouldn't be marrying until the early autumn. She would certainly go over to Galway to pay a round of visits before leaving to live at the other side of the world.

"Wouldn't it be better if Claude came to Ireland for the wedding—or even to London?" Gwen suggested. "If his family don't approve, it will be pretty dismal for you."

Maura nodded, her face shadowed.

"They'll be disappointed back home, if I don't marry in the place where I was brought up, and where most of them still live. I've godparents there. And the parish priest who christened me—he'll think it odd not to marry me."

"In that case—" Gwen began hopefully. But Maura, still frowning, explained: "It's such an expensive fare. Paul might disapprove even more if I insisted on Claude's coming back to get married— taking money out of the family business for a second trip in one year."

Gwen, who for all her kindliness and generosity, had her head screwed on very tightly indeed, felt like saying: "Since you've known each other less than two months it wouldn't hurt if you let another year go by before marrying." But this time she remembered the way her friend—her little sister, as she had come to think of her—might be feeling, so soon after her good-bye to Claude.

Instead she said placidly: "You'll have plenty of time to decide all these details—there'll be time, too, for his family to soften. What's more, with the pair of you keeping the postman busy you'll get better acquainted."

Maura looked dubious.

"I'm hopeless at letters—and Claude says he's not very good, either. Besides, if I spend my spare time writing screeds, I'll never get through my exams."

Gwen eyed her thoughtfully: "You romantic Irish have an unsuspected strain of common sense," she said.

And indeed in the months that followed, Maura worked very conscientiously. She kept the sapphire ring locked away for most of the time, and wrote to Claude once a week only. As for recreation, she cut it down so drastically that Gwen was moved to protest: to remark that neither Claude nor any other man would want to marry a girl whose head was filled, to the exclusion of all else, with medical matters.

However, when the summer came and the two of them sailed through their examinations, Maura recovered her high spirits and love of fun. She could put the magic letters S.R.N. after her name at last, and having accomplished this could look forward to marriage—a point of view which, when she explained it to Sister Foster, brought forth a very sardonic response.

"Couldn't you have made use of your training for a year or two, anyway?" she demanded. And when Maura declared earnestly that she hoped to be nursing for a while, anyway, after her marriage— that her fiancé had spoken of the great need for trained people in the Caribbean—she gave an incredulous sniff.

"Get along with you," she said. "You'll be nursing your own babies, that's what you'll be doing. Just see if I'm not correct."

Because, after a while, Claude saw more hope of

coming to Ireland for the wedding if they delayed a little, Maura continued to work at St. Matthew's, transferring now to the children's orthopaedic section. But soon after Christmas he outlined another plan. The marriage would have to take place in the West Indies after all, but in St. Jacques, where he had many good friends, not in Ste. Monique. It meant a longer journey for her, St. Jacques being two hundred miles farther on, but she would be certain to enjoy it.

Needless to say the O'Shea clan were not only disappointed but outright annoyed that she was to have what appeared to be a hole-and-corner wedding, in an island thousands of miles away, of which they had scarcely heard. They wanted to know the name of the church, the address of the priest, and her eldest brother even suggested writing out to some senior member of the Lasalle family to enquire who in God's name they thought they were, to be withholding a welcome to an O'Shea.

But Maura, by convincing her sisters that she and Claude were most truly in love, won her brothers over as well to a reluctant acceptance of the situation. In truth they could not seriously believe that these Lasalles, or anyone else for that matter, could fail to love their pretty, attractive young sister when once they came to know her. And hadn't the colleen character, as well as looks—making such easy weather of those hard examinations?

She booked her passage for a date in March on an Italian steamer which called at several exciting-sounding places on the way—at Claude's insistence travelling first-class. This settled, she embarked on a glorious shopping spree in which Gwen joined with enthusiasm.

The generosity of her family enabled her to spend

freely. They clubbed together, at the cost of some sacrifice, she felt sure, to give her a really handsome cheque—enough to cover her passage, and the cost of her trousseau with a little left over for odd expenses.

Several friends came to see her off at Waterloo, en route for Southampton, and Gwen used some of her precious off-time in travelling all the way to the docks.

It was a cold day, with a bitter east wind blowing, and everyone was envying her for sailing into the sunshine, but when the moment came at last for saying good-bye to Gwen a sudden fear assailed Maura. She felt as though she had been acting all these months in a long-drawn-out dream, and now was awakening to reality—the fact that she was going thousands of miles away from her family and friends to marry a man who in spite of his ardently affectionate letters was almost a stranger.

"Oh, Gwen," she said shakily, clinging to her friend, and crying, "I'm scared."

But though Gwen had, at the beginning of Maura's engagement, uttered words of warning, these had been so firmly disregarded that she could not now take this emotional outburst seriously.

"All brides get panicky," she consoled her. "You'll soon make friends on board—" And then she stopped short, and freed herself from Maura's clinging arms and exclaimed: "Goodness! Here's someone from my home town." And she called out to a young man who was striding purposefully towards the gangway: "Geoff! Fancy meeting you here."

The man turned and came towards the girls with a friendly smile.

"And fancy meeting you, Gwen. Don't tell me you're travelling in this ship. It would be too wonderful."

Gwen, introducing him to Maura as Geoffrey Fanshawe, explained that it was her friend who was going to the West Indies—to marry someone in St. Jacques.

"I'm getting off at Ste. Monique," he said. "St. Jacques is a good bit farther on. Still, it will be nice to have your company that far," and he eyed Maura with evident admiration. "The first day or two can be lonesome if one knows nobody."

It certainly raised Maura's spirits to have an acquaintance on board, and finding Geoffrey pleasant and friendly she listened with interest while he told Gwen of his job in the Customs Office at Ste. Monique. He had worked there for three years, it seemed, and was returning from his first leave. His parents were living in a different district now, and he had got out of touch with nearly all his old friends. He had heard that Gwen had gone to train as a nurse in London, but didn't know which hospital. Otherwise he would surely have looked her up.

Once the big white liner sailed, and Gwen's diminishing figure was out of sight, Maura went in search of her cabin. It was bright and roomy and cosily warm, and the girl with whom she was to share, and who was already unpacking, was an attractive blonde with a friendly smile.

She introduced herself as Phyllis Reeves, and in less than no time was explaining that she was going to Ste. Monique, to a splendid job as secretary and hostess at a fine new hotel there.

Maura began to feel a little disappointed that she would be living in St. Jacques, rather than Ste. Monique, after all. Of course there would have been the disadvantage that in Ste. Monique she would have been at close quarters with Claude's unwelcoming relations. Still, she had already found two congenial people in the larger island.

Claude had shown her an occasional glimpse of luxury while staying in London, but now it was a whole-time experience. The restaurant was beautifully furnished and equipped, the food delicious, and the waiters seemed really to enjoy helping the passengers to choose from the lengthy menus.

To her delight Geoffrey had arranged with the head waiter that she and Phyllis Reeves should share a table with him and another man, and this led to their forming a quartet on many other occasions.

They went ashore together in Portugal and Spain, sat together on deck, planned their costumes together for the fancy dress ball, and altogether had a great time.

Almost from the beginning they had used the bathing pool, and it was on a day of brilliant sunshine, when they were sunbathing on the boat-deck, eating a picnic lunch instead of going down to the dining-salon, when a steward brought Maura a radiogram.

Handed in at Ste. Monique, it read:

"Please disembark Ste. Monique. Lasalle."

For a moment she was startled—frightened, almost! Why should Claude make this sudden change of plan?

And then, quickly, she felt she understood. The Lasalle family had decided to welcome her after all, wanted her to have a wedding among them and their friends.

She could have ridden a high horse—declined any overtures from them. But for Claude's sake she intended to respond as warmly as she could to this last-minute gesture—forcing herself to remember that she had once thought Paul likeable, and more than that! Recalling with what affection both he and Claude had spoken of Claude's mother.

Her companions, sitting with her in the sun, were enthusiastic when she told them the contents of the radio message. Why, they would be able to come to her wedding—if she chose to invite them. It was even possible that her fiancé would after all be working, not in St. Jacques, but in Ste. Monique, so that they would be able to meet often in the future.

The ship's hostess, a charming Austrian girl who spoke English perfectly, promised to arrange matters with the people in the Purser's office, and Maura settled down to continued enjoyment of the wonderful journey, with its visits to ports and islands that had hitherto been merely glamorous names to her, and with its dances and games and cinema shows.

At last the passengers had their first view of Ste. Monique with its tree-covered mountains, and palm-fringed bays. And then, as the time drew near for landing, even those travellers who had been closest drifted apart—each looking out for the relatives and friends who had come to meet them.

For a few moments Maura stood forlornly on the quay, surrounded by her luggage, looking vainly for Claude. And in the event it was not Claude but Paul who came hurrying up, with a breathless apology for keeping her waiting.

"Where's Claude?" she exclaimed in dismay. "Is he ill? Or—or has there been an accident?"

"My car's here. We'll get it loaded up, and I'll explain," he said shortly.

"Is Claude all right?" she persisted, white beneath her tan.

He nodded.

"Just a minute while I see to the luggage."

And when they were in the car, and were driving away from the dock he told her: "I sent that cable because I couldn't possibly let you go on to St. Jacques. Claude's in Florida. He's gone back to his ex-wife."

CHAPTER 2

"ARE you telling me that your brother asked me to marry him when he had a wife already?" Maura's heart was beating to suffocation.

"Ex-wife was what I said." Paul was intent on steering his long grey car through the surging traffic. "Surely Claude told you about the divorce in Florida? About Damaris and young Peter? I'm terribly sorry for you, Maura—"

"He didn't breathe a word to me about it," Maura exclaimed fiercely. "Is it likely I would have become engaged to him if he had?"

Paul glanced round sharply at her.

"Am I to believe that Claude is an out-and-out liar? I asked him, over in London, when I saw how friendly you'd become, if he had come clean with you over the past, and he assured me that he had." He hesitated. "I was surprised at your accepting him, I must say. An Irish girl, brought up as we are over questions of divorce. I could only suppose that, like Claude—and a good many other people—you'd scrapped such old-fashioned ideas as permanency in marriage."

"Couldn't you have warned me?" she demanded bitterly. "You must surely know your brother—if anyone does."

"I didn't guess he'd go to the length of deceiving you. Anyway, I tried to get you to come out with me for a private talk, and you refused pretty brusquely. If you'd given me the chance, I could at least have told you, as my honest opinion, that Claude would sooner or later go back to Damaris. They were always fighting, and then rushing back to each other."

"But to bring me out, all these thousands of miles to the West Indies, to go through a hole-and-corner marriage somewhere—pretending all the time to love me—" Maura choked on a sob.

"I'm sure he was quite crazily keen on you," Paul said uncomfortably. "As long as he was around with you, anyway. But you're well rid of him."

"I should say so." She had recovered her voice. "It makes me sick to think I ever believed in him."

Paul swerved to avoid another car.

"He's weak, more than wicked," he said. "He fell for you on the rebound, and felt confident, I suppose, that when you landed in St. Jacques he could persuade you to marry him in the register office. Then a few days ago when Damaris wrote him a piteous letter, saying that Peter was ill and fretting for him—that she herself was heartbroken—he worked himself up into a frenzy. Confessed that you were actually on your way out to marry him, and begged me to meet you and explain—tell you how bitterly ashamed he felt over his treatment of you. So I sent that cable."

"I suppose I must thank you for stopping me from going on to St. Jacques, and for meeting me here." Maura spoke with ice in her voice. "But I'm afraid my gratitude doesn't extend very far. You and Claude haven't an ounce of real chivalry between you, and I wish with all my heart that the man who snatched my handbag, that day in London, had got away with it. Then I would never have come to know either of you."

"Once you're home again you'll quickly put us

out of your mind." Paul tried to speak reasonably. "You'll go back to your nursing, and find another, very different sort of boy-friend. Incidentally I've booked a return passage for you in a ship that leaves here in three days' time."

"That's very officious of you," she snapped. "It didn't occur to anyone so insensitive as you, I suppose, that I might not choose to go home and explain to all my friends and relations just what a fool I'd been —that they'd all been right in suggesting I was crazy to marry a man of whom I'd seen so little."

"But what are you going to do?" he demanded with a worried frown. "I'm taking you now to a very comfortable hotel, where you'll stay at my family's expense. And while you're there I'll pay for your passage and arrange a credit for you in London to cover all the expense which you've been landed in by Claude's disgraceful behaviour."

"I'll not take a cent from any of the Lasalle family." Maura's Irish temper was fairly flaring now. "I detest you all!"

"Listen, Maura. You're suffering from a terrible shock—don't know what you're saying. To-morrow when you've recovered a little, we'll have a talk."

In her agitation and distress she had scarcely noticed the crowded streets through which they were driving—conscious only of brown faces everywhere, smiling and vivacious, of big modern stores, of great trees planted here and there, aglow with bright blossoms.

Now, as they drew up before a huge white, box-like hotel, fronted by a garden full of flowering shrubs, she came to herself with a jerk.

This, she felt sure, was the new hotel where Phyllis Reeves would be working. It would be desperately humiliating to tell her what had happened, but she needed a friend so badly that she must not let this count.

"You'd better take what you want for two or three days," Paul was saying, as he opened the car for her. "I'll tote the rest of it back to the Customs shed. I arranged with the chap in charge there, who's a personal friend of mine, to do just that."

"Thank you, but I'll keep it with me," Maura returned curtly. "It's not all that much!" She could have added, "though it cost me what seems now an immense amount of wasted money," but for the life of her would not have done so. These Lasalles imagined they could make up for all her misery and heartache by arranging adequate financial compensation. They would have to learn how wrong they were.

Within a few minutes Paul, looking greatly troubled, had said good-bye to her, and gone off, with a promise to call on her next day around eleven.

In possession of a luxurious first-floor bedroom, from which she could catch a glimpse of blue, shimmering sea, Maura went automatically to the wardrobe to put away a coat she had been carrying, and was horrified by her reflection in the mirror. She could hardly believe that it was Maura O'Shea who stared back at her—white-faced and haggard, with dark shadows under her eyes.

Those weeks in London, going about with Claude to expensive restaurants, to say nothing of her recent experience of a luxury liner, had given her a certain poise. Instead of collapsing in tears, she rang the bell and asked for tea with lemon; then, refreshed, and steadied with a couple of aspirin, she went down to the bureau and asked whether she could speak to Miss Phyllis Reeves.

"She won't be on duty until to-morrow, missy," the genial hall porter told her. "But if you wish to chat with her, friendly-like, I'll get a page to show you her room."

Phyllis, already busy unpacking in her small but pleasant ground-floor bed-sitting-room, jumped to her feet as Maura came in.

"My dear, what's wrong?" she exclaimed. "Shut the door, and sit down. You look all in."

It needed every bit of self-control which Maura could muster to keep her from breaking down as she told Phyllis what had happened.

She was helped by the other girl's commonsense attitude.

"I'll leave what I think of Claude Lasalle unsaid," she commented. "The point is, what are you going to do, if you don't accept his brother's offer to send you home?"

"Stay out here for a while," was Maura's reply. "I can't face going home and telling everyone what I've just told you."

"But will you be allowed to stay? I had to sign a paper about this job, and produce documents in support of it. I suppose you made a statement that you were marrying Claude?"

Maura was taken aback for a moment. Then she said uncertainly: "Surely they'd let me stay here for a few months if I undertook nursing. Belleray's big enough for me to avoid running into Paul or his stepmother. And if Claude learns I'm here, he'll not come within miles of the island."

Phyllis pondered.

"I'm as much of a stranger here as you are," she observed. "And I'm just about as broke. Why not ring Geoffrey and explain matters to him? Get him to come round and have dinner with you this evening. He knows Ste. Monique, and could at least advise you about cheaper accommodation."

And then, before Maura could answer, she went on—just, Maura thought, as Gwen would have done: "Mind you, it's terribly foolish of you to refuse financial help from Paul. The Lasalle family owes it to you. They'd be skunks if they didn't insist on making good all you've had to waste on travelling and buying a trousseau, and the rest of it. I give this Paul good marks for that."

Maura's pale lips set in an obstinate line.

"You don't realise how I feel about Paul. I'm certain he thinks I'm not just a simpleton, promising to marry a man whom I hardly know, but a girl out to catch a good-looking chap with a reasonable income, able to give her an easy life in glamorous surroundings."

The bitterness in her voice held Phyllis silent, compassion and impatience warring in her.

After a minute or two she said evenly: "This man Paul means less than nothing to you. Why worry what he thinks? I'm sure Geoffrey, when you talk to him, will see it as I do." Adding, as Maura, stammering out her thanks to her for her kindness and sympathy, got up to go: "Maybe he'll agree with me that you're not fit, after such a shock, to come to an immediate decision—advise you to sleep on it."

When Maura got through to the *pension* where Geoffrey lived when in Belleray, he was clearly astonished to be asked to join her at dinner at the Florida-Carib Hotel.

"I can't explain over the telephone," she told him unsteadily, "but I badly want your advice. Otherwise

I shouldn't have dreamt of dragging you out on your first evening in Belleray."

"Don't worry, sweet," was his laconic response. "Expect me at eight."

He was as kind as Phyllis had been, and sitting at dinner with her in the restaurant, was soon offering some constructive help. Instead of pressing the point about accepting Paul's help, for he saw she was quite unfit for arguments, he assured her that there was a vacant room in the *Mon Abri pension* which Mrs. Perez, the proprietress, would probably be glad to let to her. It was a quiet, clean, respectable place, and far cheaper than the Florida-Carib—and his glance wandered appreciatively over the beautifully designed restaurant with its luxurious appointments—and if she liked he would have a word with Mrs. Perez, and call for her to-morrow morning to come and see the establishment for herself.

"It's not at all grand," he warned her, smiling, "but it will be a relief to be out of this palatial setting."

And later when they were sitting in a quiet corner of the spacious lounge, waiting for their coffee, he cheered her by saying that Mrs. Perez, who had lived in Ste. Monique for years and knew everybody, might be able to help her find a job.

There was a good hospital, newly built, in the town, and at least three nursing homes. It should be simple for her to find congenial work.

The coffee arrived, and the waiter was in the act of pouring it out for them—beaming at them as though they were a honeymoon couple—when Maura had a shock.

Another waiter was bringing up a visitor to her— and this was Paul.

If Maura was taken aback, so was he. But he accepted her cold invitation to join her and "my friend, Geoffrey Fanshawe"—and told her awkwardly as he drank the coffee served to him that he had looked in to see that she was comfortable and not too lonely in this vast place.

"As you're all right, I'll not stay," he said, draining his cup and setting it down. "I'll come to see you at eleven to-morrow as arranged." And giving her no chance to demur, he got up, gave them both a swift good-bye, and went striding out amid smiles and salutes from the staff, to whom he was evidently well known.

"So that's Paul Lasalle," Geoffrey observed, as he disappeared. "I know him well by sight, and by reputation, but I've never spoken to him before."

"He didn't give either of us much chance to speak to him now," Maura returned tartly. "Otherwise I'd have told him I'd probably be out to-morrow morning. But it serves him right. He takes it for granted he can override everything and everybody. He'll learn he can't do it to me."

Geoffrey smiled.

"A girl with your spirit can't be kept down!"

Maura's face clouded at that. Her blue eyes seemed very big in her white face.

"We O'Sheas are fighters," she said, "and deathly proud. But we're painfully vulnerable. And, Geoffrey," her eyes filled now with tears, "I've had a mortal wound."

He reached for her hand.

"You're a brave kid, and I'm all set to give you every bit of help I can."

Soon after eight o'clock next morning, while she

was breakfasting in her luxurious room at the Florida-Carib, Geoffrey was telephoning to her.

He had spoken to Mrs. Perez, he told her, who could let her have a small room if she would come and see it some time during the morning. There were other people after it, but if she could be there about ten, she could have the first refusal. It had only just become vacant.

"So I'll call for you and take you along in a taxi." he added. "The new car I ordered before I went on leave won't be delivered until to-morrow."

She hesitated, after thanking him, then ventured: "Did you say anything about my needing a job?"

"I did. She was sure you'd have no difficulty over finding a nursing post—of sorts. So you needn't worry about paying your way."

His cheerful, friendly voice, and the optimistic message from his landlady, did something to lighten her depression, and remove her secret fear that she had been rash in refusing to accept any compensation from Paul for the money she had spent on this wild goose chase to the Caribbean.

Hardly had she finished speaking to him than Phyllis Reeves appeared, to inquire kindly how she had slept, and if there was anything she could do for her.

She warmly agreed with Maura's plan to move as soon as she possibly could to *Mon Abri* and managed to persuade her to allow Paul to pay for her accommodation at the Florida-Carib.

"After all," she pointed out, "this is by far the most expensive hotel in Ste. Monique, and you would never have dreamt of booking in here on your own. It's elementary common sense to let him carry out the arrangement he's made with the management, to foot your bill for staying here."

Off she went, and then Paul came through on the telephone.

The travel agency had just informed him, he said, that there was a seat on the plane leaving next day for England via Bermuda. If this would suit her better than the sea voyage he would go ahead with the formalities right away—and, of course, all expenses would be his pigeon.

"You're in a great hurry to get me out of the island! I might have the plague!" Once again Maura was talking to him in freezing tones. "Small as it is, I should have thought it big enough to hold two people who dislike each other without danger of their meeting." And when he began to accuse her of childishness she broke in to say haughtily that she had already found somewhere to live and had been told she would have no difficulty in finding work as a nurse.

He was startled into silence for a moment. Then he observed stiffly that she evidently had reasons, of which he knew nothing, for wishing to remain in Ste. Monique.

"I've told you my reasons," she exclaimed, angered still more by this. "You haven't shown a glimmer of understanding."

"Perhaps I see dangers ahead to which you're blind!"

She forced a laugh.

"Don't imagine I'm the simpleton I was before I had the bad luck to meet you and your brother."

"Simpleton is an unflattering word. I prefer to say that you're very young for your age." He sounded impatient. "Otherwise you'd have the sense—yes, and the consideration for the feelings of myself and my stepmother—to let us do what we can to make up for Claude's abominable treatment of you."

"Nothing could make up for that," she snapped, near tears. "That's what partly makes me dislike you so much—your attitude that the most painful hurt can be healed by a good fat cheque."

"You're a wrong-headed, obstinate little fool." His voice fairly crackled along the telephone wire. "Because Claude has behaved like a scoundrel, you're going to take it out on the rest of the family—make us feel like worms, by refusing to accept any sort of financial compensation."

"I can understand it's giving you a shock, discovering I'm not a gold-digger!" There was nothing very youthful in her searing sarcasm. "You thought I was that, no doubt, when I became engaged to your brother."

"You're impossible!" he exploded. "An absolute little vixen. Why vent your bitterness on my stepmother and myself? We only want to help you—show you in concrete form how distressed and shamed we are."

"You can help me best by leaving me in peace," Maura said, her wrath suddenly dying down into inexpressible weariness. "I'll be grateful if you'll pay my bill here. It isn't the sort of place I could ever have afforded. But that's all. Good-bye."

And with that she hung up the receiver.

The drive with Geoffrey to *Mon Abri* gave her a clearer picture of Belleray, the capital of the island. Green hills, tree-covered, ringed Saint's Bay, with its busy harbour, and from these had been carved roads on which stood houses of varying size and shape, washed in pale tints of blue and pink and jade, interspersed here and there with a large, box-like modern building. Many of the houses had bright gardens, for up here was the residential section. But even in the business quarter, in the streets level with the sea-front, great flowering trees brought tropical brilliance to the scene; and the gay clothes of the passers-by, brown-skinned for the most part, lent a further exotic note.

"It's wonderfully beautiful," Maura murmured, stabbed with the thought that if her expectations had been fulfilled she would have been making her home in one of these sunny islands, set in a turquoise sea.

Geoffrey nodded.

"But it has its disadvantages. Huge ants which ravage the gardens. Roaches which make their appearance in the cleanest houses."

"No worse, I suppose, than our slugs and snails—and mice!"

"Maybe not. And anyway we have the sun—kept from scorching us up by the blessedly cool trade winds."

Mon Abri was in a street half-way up the hillside, with a view across the bay to the tiny island of Tapoco; it was small and compact, with a garden filled with shrubs blossoming in red and yellow.

A brown-complexioned maid, in cap and apron, answered their ring with a smile, and showed them into a tiny back room which evidently served as bed-sitting-room and office, where Mrs. Perez was working at her desk.

She was a wiry little woman with wavy grey hair and black, darting eyes, and she gave them a brisk welcome, taking Maura at once to see a small room on the second floor, sparsely, even shabbily furnished, but spotlessly clean.

She quoted a modest sum, to include breakfast and supper, and explained that these were her lowest terms.

"I'm keeping the price down because you're a friend of Mr. Fanshawe, who is a most kind and helpful tenant," she said, "and because he tells me that you are not settled in a job yet. But I must ask you to make up your mind at once and, if you want it, to pay one week's rent in advance."

Maura, relieved to have found accommodation at a reasonable rental, arranged to move in that afternoon and went back to join Geoffrey in the little office.

A difficulty occurred because she had as yet no West Indian currency, but Geoffrey produced the necessary money, promising to take her to the bank he himself used, in order to change some English pounds.

"I hear you want to find work as a nurse, Miss O'Shea." Mrs. Perez, having locked the money away without comment, came back from her desk and sat down. "I may be able to help you there."

"The sooner the better," was Maura's quick response.

"Well, there's a Mrs. Martin, and her niece, Raymonde Sorel, both with some hospital training, who have opened a small nursing home five minutes' walk from here."

Maura's keen ears took in, with faint apprehension, the phrase—"some hospital training"—but she said nothing, listening attentively.

"They've been going more than a year now, but are always complaining of shortage of staff," Mrs. Perez went on. "They tell me this when they drop in to visit with me sometimes. You see, before they started their home, they stayed here in two of my best rooms, and I got to know them quite well."

"Are they doing all right?" Maura asked, feeling rather bold in asking such a question.

But Mrs. Perez was not in the least offended.

"Quite well, so far as I know!"

"Then would you be so very kind as to give me an introduction to them?"

Mrs. Perez returned to her desk and took up the telephone.

"I'll put you in touch with Mrs. Martin right away," she said. "And I'm certain she'll jump at the chance of getting a State-registered nurse, straight from England."

This proved to be the case. A very short conversation with Mrs. Martin ended by Maura finding herself engaged to start work the very next morning on a temporary basis, at a fair salary.

"On our side we don't want to bother with a preliminary interview," Mrs. Martin told her heartily. "If we take to each other we can come to a permanent arrangement. This is just a trial run."

After a visit to the bank, Geoffrey took her back to the Florida-Carib to collect her luggage, and she heard then that Paul Lasalle had called to see her.

It was Phyllis Reeves, established at a typewriter in the office now, who told her—adding that he had seemed very put out at missing her and had left a telephone number with the request that she would ring him up some time during the day.

"I can't think why you dislike him so much, Maura," she added under her breath, with a watchful eye cocked on the manager. "He's extremely attractive, and very distinguished-looking."

Maura could have said with truth: "I thought so

once—liked him far better than his brother—could have fallen for him, in fact, in a big way!" But she hated to admit this even to herself now, and merely observed shortly that she found him intolerable, and hoped sincerely that she would never come into contact with him again.

Phyllis smiled sympathetically.

"So long as you keep in touch with me, Maura," she said, "I'd worry if you didn't," adding mischievously: "But mind you don't go for Geoffrey. I've my eye on that lad myself!"

Before leaving the hotel for good Maura broke her resolution to ignore Paul's message, and rang him up, unable to resist telling him that she had already found excellent accommodation—and a job.

But she quickly regretted her impulse. Paul hit back at once.

"It's very odd to me," he said pugnaciously, "that you should be so set on staying in Ste. Monique. You know perfectly well that you're bound to run into Claude sooner or later."

"I know nothing of the kind," she retorted hotly. "Whether he intends to work in Florida or St. Jacques, he'll be hundreds of miles from here."

"Where his mother happens to live!" he snapped. "A mother to whom he's devoted, whatever his faults—whom he visits constantly."

"Ste. Monique is big enough for me to avoid any member of the Lasalle family," she told him haughtily.

"I doubt it. If you are determined to stay in the West Indies, why don't you go on to Raballo? It's far bigger, with much better opportunities for trained nurses."

"Because I have friends here," she said stiffly. "I've

no desire to go to an island where I know nobody."

"Your friend Mr. Fanshawe has certainly arranged things for you in Ste. Monique with remarkable speed" was his sarcastic response to this; and then he added sharply: "Maybe he's the reason for your wanting to hang around Ste. Monique. You must have *some* deep motive! And I must say I'd rather he was the lure than my painfully weak brother."

"What are you daring to imply?" She could hardly get the words out for anger.

But the line had gone dead. She could only hang up the receiver and rejoin Geoffrey in the hotel vestibule.

CHAPTER 3

MAURA awoke early with the sunshine flooding her little top room, and the sound of cocks crowing and dogs yapping in her ears.

For a moment she could not remember where she was. She had been dreaming that she was in the Italian liner playing deck quoits with Paul—of all people—as her partner: playing against the ship's stout doctor and the attractive Austrian hostess. An absurd but happy dream.

Now, back in reality, her spirits sagged.

All too clearly she recalled, still with a sense of shock, that meeting with Paul on the quayside; his telling her curtly, that Claude had not come to welcome her as his bride-to-be because he had returned to his ex-wife.

Had Paul been gentler, what a difference it would have made. As it was, his first supposition that she was well aware of Claude's previous marriage, knew of Damaris and the little boy, was salt in the terrible wound that Claude had dealt her. And then his idea that the best way to treat her was to make full financial compensation for the expenses she had incurred, coming out to the Caribbean, and pack her back to England on the first boat or plane—even suggesting that she should return to the hospital where she had been working.

She tried to brace up her will—to remind herself that she was lucky in the friendships she had made on board ship. Geoffrey Fanshawe, who had persuaded

Mrs. Perez to let her have a room in the *pension* where he himself lived. Phyllis Reeves, starting a heavy job in the office of the Florida-Carib Hotel, yet finding time to assure her of her help when she needed it, of her friendship.

But always that nightmare meeting with Paul recurred, blotting out every other thought or memory.

Lying there under the mosquito net she wrenched her mind to the immediate future, and found herself hoping that this job at Mrs. Martin's nursing home would prove a strenuous one.

The pay was good, and she was to have most of her meals at the home, so she would surely be able to save regularly. And perhaps after a while Gwen would come out to the West Indies, and get her cousins in Raballo to find jobs for them both out there. It would be wonderful to be working with Gwen again, or at any rate in the same hospital.

Somewhere a clock struck four, and she plumped up her pillow and tried to go to sleep again. Breakfast, Mrs. Perez had said, would be served at seven; and her appointment at the nursing home was for an hour later. Wakeful as she felt, there was no point in getting up just yet.

To her surprise she became extremely drowsy, and this time was aroused at six o'clock by someone at a near-by church ringing out the Angelus on a cracked bell. A cool shower in the tiny, shabby bathroom—so different from the luxurious ones on board ship and in the Florida-Carib—refreshed her. And at breakfast, greeted cheerfully by Geoffrey, and then by Mrs. Perez who introduced her to the other guests, she found she had a healthy appetite for the sweet juicy grapefruit and excellent coffee and rolls.

Here again the table appointments presented something of a contrast to those to which she had lately become accustomed. But what did that matter? *Mon Abri* was just the right sort of establishment for a girl on her own, earning a living.

Mrs. Martin's nursing home, Hillside, proved less ordinary than its name. A long, low structure, set in a bright garden, it had none of the shabbiness of *Mon Abri*, and had evidently been built far more recently: probably, she thought, as she passed through the wrought-iron gate, within the last few years.

A young maid, hardly more than a schoolgirl, gave her the usual flashing smile, and took her straight to Mrs. Martin's office—again very much larger and smarter than the room which Mrs. Perez dignified by that term.

And Mrs. Martin herself was very much larger and smarter than the chatelaine of *Mon Abri*.

A woman in, Maura guessed, her middle fifties, she was spotlessly dressed in white—overall, stockings and shoes—and her fashionably set, cleverly tinted auburn hair and well-corseted figure proclaimed her prosperity.

Her manner was pleasant but without warmth, and she lost no time in "re-capping" the terms she had laid down to Maura on the telephone.

Only one thing about the arrangements troubled Maura. The salary, like the time off, was generous, but it was payable on the last day of each month, and she wondered how, having agreed to Mrs. Perez' request for payment in advance, she was going to manage on the small amount of money she now possessed.

She had come to Hillside intending to ask for a small advance, but there was something about Mrs.

Martin that discouraged the idea. She would probably regard as inefficient a girl who came to look for work in a strange country without sufficient resources to tide her over a few weeks.

"If she knew my circumstances, she might even offer a 'sub'," she thought. But she shrank from baring her wounds to this rather hard-faced stranger. She had confided her heartbreaking experiences and her consequent difficulties only to Phyllis and Geoffrey, who had promised to keep things to themselves. She would be well advised to maintain a similar silence, and eke out her money as best she could.

The nursing home was laid out on one floor in the form of an open square, the courtyard in the centre being crossed by concrete paths, and like the outer garden, gay with flowering shrubs. There were three bedrooms for patients on each side of the square, and Maura saw at once, as Mrs. Martin took her on a tour of inspection, that the place would be easy to run and, with its verandas and French windows, delightfully fresh and airy.

As she had expected, the equipment was far below the standards of a London hospital. Still, she felt sure that it was as good as that of many an English nursing home of the same size catering, as did Hillside, for medical cases only.

She was halfway round before she encountered Mrs. Martin's niece, Raymonde Sorel, who, coming out of a sickroom, greeted her with more surprise than cordiality.

"You're very young," she observed, her dark eyes faintly disapproving. "I imagined someone older—and more experienced—if you don't mind my saying so."

"Not in the least." A sure instinct told Maura that

she would have to stand up to this tall, handsome brunette, elegant even in her simple white overall. "I'm a State-registered nurse, and since I took my finals I've been working in the big London hospital where I qualified." She turned to Mrs. Martin and observed: "I didn't mention my age, since you didn't ask it, but I'm in my early twenties."

"Oh, Raymonde wasn't criticising you," Mrs. Martin said quickly—and Maura caught the tail-end of a warning look which she shot at her niece. "We're very glad to have you. And now you've seen the layout, I'm going to introduce you to some of your patients."

There were heart cases, diabetics, a man with severe asthma, and two women with arthritis. Under a good doctor she could tackle any of them, Maura thought, wondering how far she could rely on Mrs. Martin and Raymonde for help in an emergency.

It was essential to know what qualifications they possessed, but she could hardly ask straight out. She would have to wait for enlightenment until the first time she spoke to one of the visiting doctors.

She had brought her uniform from England, thinking that for a while after her marriage she might undertake some private nursing, and she had dressed herself in this before leaving *Mon Abri* that morning.

Mrs. Martin clearly approved—indeed she said frankly that she was proud to have people know that she had a nurse from such a distinguished hospital as St. Matthew's. But Raymonde's offhand comment was that Miss O'Shea would soon find her grand English uniform unpractical in the tropics and be glad to adopt the simple overall and veil which she and her aunt were wearing.

Although Maura knew that Raymonde was probably right, she so resented her way of speaking that she resolved obstinately to use her own uniform as long as she could.

Why should this older girl be so cold and unfriendly? Was she jealous? And if so, just why?

As the days went by she grasped the reason. Whatever training Mrs. Martin might or might not have had, she was a good practical nurse. But Raymonde was not only ignorant, but careless, especially over matters of hygiene.

"Shades of Sister Foster!" she thought as, from the corner of her eye, she saw her administering medicine with an unwashed spoon, or making up a bed with sheets that looked suspiciously as though they had been used before—if only for a patient who had spent a single night in the home, for observation.

For a couple of weeks she said nothing, hoping that Raymonde, who was obviously intelligent, would notice and follow her own scrupulous methods. And she dropped not the least hint of her perplexity to Mrs. Perez or to Geoffrey, when she went back every evening to *Mon Abri*.

In her off-time she wanted to forget Hillside and its problems, and in this she was helped by Geoffrey and Phyllis, who invited her to join them in picnics and drives, a man from Geoffrey's office or a lonely tourist at the Florida-Carib making up a fourth.

A young doctor who visited the home, Alan Field, also asked her to go out with him, when she had been working there three weeks, but this overture she firmly refused. If she began going out with any of the Hillside doctors Raymonde would have added cause for jealousy. And apart from this, while it was restful to go around with Geoffrey and Phyllis and their friends after work, she was still too raw and sore from

Claude's treatment of her, and from Paul's lack of tact and sympathy, to want the company of a solitary male, however agreeable.

Towards the end of the month, the surface calm of Hillside was rudely ruffled.

Maura caught sight of Raymonde preparing to give an injection with a needle which she knew had not been sterilised, and protested strongly.

Raymonde's reply, as she walked out of the little white-tiled surgery where they had both been working, was a curt, "Mind your own business," and this made Maura carry out her resolution to report any gross carelessness to Mrs. Martin.

Off she went to the office where Mrs. Martin was usually to be found at this hour and told her, as a matter of urgency, the kind of thing that had been happening—the unsterilised needle being the last straw.

Mrs. Martin listened in silence and then said quietly that she would speak to her niece and impress on her once again the vital need for absolute cleanliness—in the medical sense.

On this, Maura turned to go, but Mrs. Martin put out a detaining hand.

"I'm going to give you a confidence," she said, in a more friendly tone than she had yet used to Maura. "Raymonde's training doesn't amount to much—it wouldn't, anyway, in the eyes of the staff of St. Matthew's—and what is more, she doesn't really care for nursing."

"Then why does she do it?" Maura demanded, her blue eyes wide open.

"She thought she was going to like it, and invested her small savings in this place," was Mrs. Martin's explanation. "It would be difficult for me to return a lump sum to her just now—I've sunk so much capital in building costs and equipment. Also—" and she hesitated, "I think Raymonde might find a husband from among the doctors visiting here. She's good-looking and attractive—"

"I'll say she is," Maura exclaimed. "Really beautiful, when she takes trouble over herself."

"But not everyone's idea of a wife," Mrs. Martin commented. And with a short: "This is all in strict confidence, please," she gave Maura to understand that the interview was at an end.

During the next few days she noticed that Raymonde, though even more sullen in her manner to her, was considerably more careful over sterilisation.

However, at the very end of her first four weeks when, very short indeed of cash, she was looking forward to receiving her salary, peace at Hillside was again shattered.

Raymonde had gone off for the day, and she was attending to her patients, when Dr. Field arrived, to visit a woman with thrombosis. Maura had not yet got round to her when Dr. Field asked stiffly if he might speak to her alone—and at once.

"I understood you were a fully trained nurse," he said, with barely controlled anger.

"So I am," she returned quickly.

"Then how is it that Mrs. Randall has bed-sores?" he snapped. "I've not been round for three days—been in bed with fever—and this is what I find."

It was on the tip of Maura's tongue to retort that Mrs. Randall was not one of her patients, but that she had warned Nurse Sorel a week ago, after doing duty for her, to be particularly careful over this case.

Suddenly recalling, however, that conversation with Mrs. Martin, she bit back the words, and in a way which Sister Foster would undoubtedly have approved, said quietly that she was very sorry indeed that this had happened, and would attend to Mrs. Randall within the next few minutes.

Dr. Field gave her a considering look and seemed about to say something further—to ask her a question, she suspected—but evidently thinking better of it, he merely shrugged his shoulders and went his way.

CHAPTER 4

THIS incident marked a slight improvement in Raymonde's behaviour to Maura. True, she denied all responsibility for Mrs. Randall's condition, putting all the blame on a young nursing auxiliary who, she declared, had disobeyed her orders. But she expressed appreciation, in her curt, offhand way, for Maura's acceptance of blame which she did not in the least deserve, and actually suggested that they should take some time off together if and when a chance presented itself. Go shopping, perhaps.

Maura smiled and nodded, feeling comfortably sure that the occasion when they could both be away from Hillside during daylight hours would never occur. But one afternoon when there was a gap between the departure of several patients and the arrival of others, Mrs. Martin insisted on taking over and sending the two of them off. She and the young nursing auxiliary could very well manage.

In possession now of a month's salary, for Mrs. Martin had paid her with meticulous promptness, Maura was quite pleased to go round the shops with someone who knew Belleray so well. She didn't intend to spend very much, but she wanted to follow up her short, unhappy letters to her family in Galway and to Gwen, with some postcards showing the beauties of Ste. Monique—to assure them that she was in a good job, and reasonably cheerful.

Raymonde's purchases were more extensive, and involved trailing round innumerable shops, large and small, in search of material for two new dresses, and by the time she had found what she wanted, and they were emerging into the main street, they were both ready to drop.

It was at this moment that Maura caught sight of Paul Lasalle, his big car caught in a traffic jam. She would have pretended not to see him, though he was so close to the kerb that she could have touched him, but Raymonde, with an exclamation: "Paul! How marvellous to see you. My friend and I are dead beat. Be an angel and run us home."

He looked round, and without a change of expression, said crisply: "Jump in, both of you. We'll be moved on in a minute."

Maura, taken aback completely, hesitated, but Raymonde, with a: "Quick, for goodness' sake," bundled her into the back of the car, she herself nipping into the front seat by Paul.

He reached to shut both doors and had scarcely done so when the traffic moved on, and then he asked evenly what Raymonde meant by home—if Maura was also living at Hillside.

"She's working with me there, but living at a *pension* near by," Raymonde told him. "If you'll drop us at Hillside she can easily walk to *Mon Abri*, can't you, Maura?"

"Very easily," Maura returned, trying to sound cool and composed as Raymonde went on gaily: "You must come in and have a rum-and-ginger ale with us, Paul. It's ages since we've seen you."

But when they reached Hillside, Paul made a charming apology for not staying there, and insisted so blandly but so firmly on taking Maura on to *Mon Abri* that she could have hardly refused his offer without exciting surprised comment.

And though he started in the direction of the *pension* he very soon changed course, taking a road to the hills.

"Where are we going?" she asked sharply.

"For a little drive. The air is fresher up there. You're paler than you were when you first came to Ste. Monique."

"I don't wish to go driving with you," she snapped. "You insulted me beyond bearing the last time I spoke to you on the telephone—actually implying that I was hanging about in Ste. Monique in the hope of seeing Claude again."

"I'm sorry. I lost my temper, Maura. You can be pretty maddening, you know."

"So can you." And then she added, indignation bubbling up in her again: "As if I'd wish to speak to Claude again, ever—and he a married man with a child!"

"They haven't remarried legally yet," Paul pointed out. "And whether he'd hold to his resolution if he met you again, I'm none too sure. I'm not trying to pay you fulsome compliments when I tell you that you're a far more attractive girl than Damaris, hot temper, silly pride and all."

"I'm not interested in comparisons between Claude's ex-wife and myself," was her lofty response. "Nor, in fact, in anything else you can say to me. So maybe it would be sensible for you to turn the car as soon as you can, and take me to my *pension*."

"It's not possible to turn on this road for at least a mile—not with safety, at least. So you might just as well listen to me. It's this, Maura. Mrs. Martin is in a very rocky state, financially. It's well known in Belleray that she's in debt all round."

"Then she has my sympathy," Maura retorted.

"And mine—up to a point. Not being a business woman she gaily ignored the warning which responsible people in Belleray gave her about the danger of starting a project with insufficient capital." He paused, then went on: "It's said she economises in rather odd ways. Keeps her staff waiting weeks for their meagre salaries—which is most unfair, even if they aren't properly trained."

"Belleray seems to be a hive of gossip," Maura commented scornfully. "Speaking for myself, Mrs. Martin pays me well and promptly. I've no complaints."

"New brooms—to alter the proverb a little—are carefully used. And as a fully qualified nurse you have special value. Let's hope your contentment continues, that's all."

She made no answer to this, and at the first widening of the narrow, twisting road, he manoeuvred the car round, and with the engine still running, stopped.

"You see that house over there," he said casually, indicating a low white house of considerable size in the distance. "That's our family home, where my stepmother lives—and I, too, except when I have to spend the night in town. If things had been different I'd—I'd have liked to show it to you."

"If things had been different?" she repeated slowly.

"Yes. If you hadn't fallen for Claude!"

"In that case I should hardly be here in Ste. Monique," she pointed out shortly. Then, with a sudden surge of grief and anger, she rounded on him: "Why must you keep reminding me of the unhappiest, most humiliating experience of my life? Of a man who is nothing to me but an ugly memory—mercifully, a rapidly fading one?"

He looked down at her, but her face was averted.

He could see only the sweet line of her cheek—and a large tear coursing down.

"I'm sorry," he said once again, and started on the downward road towards *Mon Abri*.

She found Geoffrey alone, sitting on a bench in the little garden, and went to join him. Though Phyllis was his unofficial girl-friend, he and Maura, living in the same *pension*, naturally saw a good deal of each other, and he sometimes reminded her, when she looked tired and worried after a hard day at Hillside, of his promise to come to her help should she ever need it.

Now, more disturbed than she had allowed Paul to guess, she summoned up the courage to ask Geoffrey, in absolute confidence, if he had ever heard any rumours that Mrs. Martin's financial position was precarious.

He gave her a cigarette and lit it for her.

"Sheer nonsense," he said. "It's true she started on an almost ridiculously small amount of capital, but she's doing fine now. Or so I hear!"

"Then she's not overwhelmed with debts?"

He looked at her with a puzzled, slightly resentful expression.

"Who's been getting at you? She has bills to pay off, of course—to builders and decorators, and so on. But, as you know, Hillside has plenty of patients paying hefty fees—"

"I've no idea what anyone pays," Maura said quickly. "And I'm only too glad there's nothing to worry about. Mrs. Martin is obviously a very brave woman."

Geoffrey nodded, and squeezed her hand reassuringly.

"Don't listen to all the rumours you hear, my dear. And don't—just because you've been treated abominably by one rogue—imagine there is danger round every corner."

Raymonde came strolling along the road just then, and called to Maura that it was nearly time to go back to Hillside for a spell of duty.

Invited to come in for a moment, she accepted nonchalantly.

"What did you think of our Maiden's Dream?" she demanded, dropping into a wicker chair. "And why didn't you lure him in for a drink? I found I was too early for work, so walked up expecting to see his car outside."

"Maura thinks nothing of Paul Lasalle," Geoffrey interrupted, scowling. "He's the last person she'd invite to come in."

"So you knew him already! You're a dark horse!" There was sharp hostility as well as surprise in Raymonde's dark eyes. "Well, whether you like or loathe him you must have let him take you for a pretty long drive. I thought you must have made a quick conquest when I got here and found you were still out."

"And now you know you're wrong," Maura returned evenly. She glanced at her watch. "If you'll give me a few minutes for a shower and change, I'll be ready to start with you for Hillside."

She well knew as she left Geoffrey and Raymonde sitting together in the garden that Raymonde would lose no time in starting pumping operations, but she felt certain that she wouldn't learn much. In any case, what was the use of worrying? She must concentrate on earning the money to take her home, doing her best for her patients, and enjoying as far as she could the beauties of this island paradise. Meanwhile, though people might talk and get everything wrong, what did it matter? As the folk at home would have said, if you had a good conscience you could look anyone in the eye. And most surely she had done nothing to be ashamed of.

In fact, Maura had less to worry about on the score of gossip than she realised. But for Claude's secrecy over his engagement to her the whole island would have been agog with the story. As it was, only Geoffrey Fanshawe and Phyllis Reeves—and, of course, the Lasalles—knew precisely what had happened. For among the other passengers who had disembarked there were none with whom she had had more than the slightest acquaintance—if that. To them she had just been one of the many pretty girls on board who had spent her time with a small set of congenial passengers of her own age.

Raymonde was certainly curious—the more so because of Geoffrey's oyster-like attitude. Scenting a broken romance between Maura and Paul, she began to put out feelers when alone with Maura—a form of annoyance which Maura, though so much younger and, by nature, so much franker, managed to deal with by sheer Irish quick-wittedness.

Only once, when Raymonde mentioned Claude's name in connection with his divorce from Damaris and his reconciliation with her, did Maura lose, for a second, her apparent serenity. But Raymonde, far more interested in her feelings for Paul, did not even notice that moment of disquiet.

With time slipping by Maura found herself thinking less and less of Claude and, though she saw nothing of him, more and more of his extremely irritating brother.

And then one free afternoon, when she was coming

out of the Public Library on the same block as the Florida-Carib Hotel, she ran slap into Claude.

She would have cut him dead, but his voice, as he murmured, "Maura, give me one minute to ask your pardon," was so bitterly ashamed, and so unhappy, that she stopped, though only to tell him quietly that she had nothing to say to him.

"I only want you to say one thing—that you forgive me." He laid his hand gently on her arm. "And to explain my disgraceful behaviour to you—even if it makes you hate me more than ever."

"Hate is something I know nothing about, thank God!" Her eyes had begun to brim with tears. "That would mean wishing you ill, and I've never done that to anybody."

"I hate myself, Maura. When I think that I might have caused you to—to commit suicide—!"

She blinked back her tears at that.

"With all your apologies you've too good an opinion of yourself, Claude," she exclaimed, contemptuous now, and the Irish way of speech coming back to her tongue. "Is it kill myself because some rascal behaved like a cad to me? Be yourself, boyo—thinking yourself worth dying for!"

They had reached the bus stop a few yards from the Florida-Carib now, and the next minute she was hopping on to the small single-seater bus that went up to the district where both Hillside and *Mon Abri* were situated.

She was unaware until she got out near the *pension* that Claude had followed her into the bus. Nor that Paul, emerging from the Florida-Carib with Phyllis Reeves, had been a furious witness of the episode.

Angry as she was with Claude, Maura could hardly shake him off in the street without creating a scene, and determined not to introduce him at *Mon Abri* she suggested icily that they should go for a cup of coffee into a near-by café down a side road, so poor and shabby that she knew there was no chance of encountering any of her acquaintances there.

And there, in a quiet corner, Claude told her of his shame and penitence.

When he had first met her, just after his divorce had gone through, he had not imagined for a moment that there would be any question for him of returning to Damaris.

"I fell in love with you, as I'd never been in love before," he said, and when she tried to stop him saying such things, he insisted almost wildly that she must let him get everything off his chest—promising that after this evening he would never attempt to speak to her again.

"I knew very well that if I told you about Damaris and Peter, you'd send me packing," he went on. "But I thought that if I took time to make you care deeply for me, so that the idea of parting from me would seem—well, an impossibility—your narrow-minded prejudices would melt."

"Narrow-minded prejudices!" she repeated, with a lift of her eyebrows. "You'd got a bit far from your early upbringing, Claude—you with a child, and all! No wonder you didn't want to come over to Ireland for our wedding!"

"I know. It was infamous of me to bring you out here, in the hope of persuading you to marry me all in a hurry, in a hole-and-corner way."

"It would have been a totally vain hope." Maura, her coffee finished, took up her bag. "And now, Claude, I must go—with just one word to you. You've been given this chance to make a fresh start with your wife and little boy—and the luck not to break my heart. But don't try tempting Providence again."

"Won't you let me explain what sent me back to Damaris?" he pleaded, and though she shook her head, unwilling to listen any more, he went on, under his breath, in a rush of words, "It wasn't simply and solely that Damaris was desperately anxious to try again—admitting that it was partly her fault—nor even that Peter was ill and fretting for me. It was my own sudden realisation that Mother and Paul were right—that marriage is far too serious a tie to be broken by two people behaving like spoilt children. That I hadn't given mine a chance."

She made another move to go, having no comment to make on this self-evident truth, but he went on, after the briefest hesitation: "Paul even said—and you mustn't be hurt and angry, Maura—that my crazy feeling for you was simply infatuation, that would burn itself out: that real love puts the good of the loved one first. And yet—oh, *Maura*—!"

"That's enough," she said imperiously, getting quickly to her feet. "Good-bye, Claude." And with that she left him.

For all her apparent composure that encounter with Claude had shaken her badly. She was very far from loving him—indeed she despised him for his flabbiness. But she was contemptuous of herself as well for having given her heart to a cheat, a weakling. Couldn't she have found a man on whom to pour out affection, instead of on this irresponsible playboy?

And then she reproached herself for being hard and intolerant. Maybe, after all this trouble and misery, he would make a go of it with Damaris. Maybe he had learnt his bitter lesson.

As for herself she was heart-free—and maybe, some day, would be happy again.

She made her way very slowly to the *pension*, very tired, and hoping to reach the sanctuary of her attic bedroom without meeting any of the residents. But Mrs. Perez, hearing her step, came out of her office, holding a slip of paper.

"Mr. Lasalle has just rung up," she said. "He wants you to dine with him, and on the chance that you are not otherwise engaged will be calling for you at eight o'clock."

Maura flushed with annoyance.

"You can tell Claude Lasalle, if he rings again—" she began, but Mrs. Perez interrupted her.

"Not Claude Lasalle," she said, with a puzzled look. "It was Mr. Paul who rang. And it didn't sound a very cordial invitation, I must say. He made me repeat his message word for word, so that I got it right—insisting on that bit about 'otherwise engaged.'"

Maura's head swam. So he knew, somehow, of her meeting with Claude. She already had a headache. Should she make this a pretext for going to bed very early, and so avoid seeing him? Or should she, guessing what he must be thinking, put him in his place for all time?

After a moment or two of hesitation Maura decided to have it out with Paul for good and all.

Whether he had seen her with Claude, or whether someone else had noticed them together and told him about it, she did not know. But she was certain that her meeting with his brother was the reason for this chilly invitation.

He would misjudge her, of course, even accusing her, perhaps, of coming between Claude and his former wife, crushing all hopes of their permanent reconciliation.

Having braced herself, tired and overwrought as she was, to this most distasteful interview with Paul, she went up to her little attic room to change, choosing a plain dark blue dress lightened with a string of white-and-blue beads which her friend Gwen had given her as a parting present when she left England for this journey to the Caribbean. A journey begun so happily and ending in such dismay and sorrow.

If she had dressed up, worn something more elaborate, Paul would take it for granted that she expected him to entertain her at some expensive restaurant in Belleray. And this was the last thing she wanted. A small, quiet place, where it would be impossible to spend much money on her—that was what she intended to stipulate as a condition of going out with him. Disliking him as she did, she wasn't allowing him to patronise her—playing the rich man to the poor little nurse.

She need not have worried on this score. As soon as he arrived in his powerful car, and she came out to meet him, he asked her coolly if she had any objection to dining at a small restaurant in Clombières, a fishing village a few miles away.

"It's essential that we have a straight talk," he said. "And out there we shan't be likely to run into anyone we know."

She was so utterly exhausted, physically, mentally and emotionally, and the car, with its silent driver, ran so smoothly through the darkness, that in a short while she dropped off to sleep. The lapping of the tideless sea on the beaches of the little bays which the winding coast road skirted did not reach her, nor did she feel the cool night breeze on her face.

But as the car slid gently to a standstill and, hunched in her seat, as far as possible from Paul, she slipped from deep sleep into semi-waking, she had the strangest notion, lasting only for a split second, that a man's lips had brushed hers, in the lightest of light kisses.

She struggled up, forgetting for an instant where she was. She must, of course, have been dreaming. There was Paul, standing in the moonlight, on the far side of the car, and as he came round to open the door on her side, his face was as sombre and aloof as always.

In any case what crazy folly to imagine even so briefly—when half awake—that Paul, of all men she had ever met, Paul who detested and despised her, would have acted so out of character as to brush her lips with his.

Deeply thankful that he could not read her stupid, shaming thoughts, she got out of the car and went with him into the restaurant, over the door of which hung a sign: "The Three Fishers."

Floor and tables were of plain, scrubbed wood, and the whitewashed walls were decorated with fishing-net draperies and spears, and old hurricane lamps.

It was not quite the humble establishment she would have preferred. There were two tables seating American tourists, and most of the local patrons seemed, by all the sounds, to have foregathered in the bar, a short way beyond.

But there was no crowding of tables—that might come later when the restaurant became better known

—and it was possible to talk without danger of other customers overhearing.

For a while, eating delicious flying fish, Maura and Paul talked trivialities. Then while waiting for the next course, Paul said, speaking with an effort, "It gave me a terrible shock, Maura, to see you and Claude together—and going off in the same bus. I didn't know that you were even aware of his being in Ste. Monique for a few hours."

She stiffened.

"I had no idea he was here."

"Rather a coincidence, wasn't it, running into him like that? And a pity, from your point of view, that it had to happen so near the Florida-Carib. As you know, I use that hotel a lot—almost like a club, in fact, when I'm in Belleray."

"Are you accusing me of lying?" Maura had gone very white. Her blue eyes were enormous in her heart-shaped face—and their expression was furiously angry.

He avoided a direct answer.

"Can't you see how it looks to me?" he demanded. "You must have a strong motive for staying out here in Ste. Monique, working in a tropical climate in a potty little nursing home where you can't even be sure of a regular salary."

"That last remark is a libel on Mrs. Martin," Maura snapped. "She pays me generously, and on the dot."

"I hope it will go on that way," was Paul's dry comment. "Let's go back to your motive in staying on here. Isn't it in the hope—a very natural hope, I suppose—that Claude will at least give you his own version of his conduct to you? After all, you only heard at second-hand—from me—that he was going back to his wife and child!"

She looked at him for a moment in silence. Then she said slowly: "That would be a good many degrees less shameful than trying to persuade him to stick to his engagement to me instead of returning to Damaris and Peter—the accusation I've learned to expect from you."

"I'm sorry—very sorry—if I've misjudged you, Maura! But don't you see that even to meet Claude by design is dangerous?"

"It was his design, not mine," she retorted hotly. "And it's hypocritical nonsense on your part saying you're sorry for all these false accusations you've made against me. Your one idea is to get me out of the islands, and you don't care what stick you use in your efforts to drive me away."

"We're getting off the point," Paul said steadily. "If Claude knows you're out here, and keeps seeing you, Damaris won't have a chance to hold him. You're far more attractive than she is—and he is as weak as water."

"You misjudge him, too," Maura told him. "He made up his mind to see me by hook or crook. Lay in wait for me—and I not even knowing he was in the island." She paused, then went on sombrely: "He wanted me to forgive him for the way he behaved to me—seemed deeply sorry and ashamed."

"So he should be," Paul exclaimed indignantly. And then he continued, in a different tone: "Even so, Maura—and I'm saying this because I know Claude so well—it would be asking for trouble to let him get into the way of seeing you every time he came to Ste. Monique. It's true he'll be working in St. Jacques —settled down, one hopes, with Damaris and Peter for good. But he won't be all that far away—by air, anyway—and he'll have to come here sometimes for conferences, and to visit his mother."

"You'd better encourage him to bring his wife and child with him," Maura returned shortly. "In any case, I told him definitely this afternoon, in a way he couldn't misunderstand, that it was good-bye—that I never wanted to see him, or speak to him, again." She hesitated a moment, then went on, looking him straight in the eyes: "That goes for you, too, Paul. Ste. Monique is big enough to hold us both. If we do have to meet, it can be more or less as strangers."

"That's one degree better than meeting as enemies," he said, smiling faintly. "We might even in the course of time, if you stayed out here long enough, learn to be friends."

"But you don't want me to remain in the Caribbean," she commented drily. "And I certainly shan't —indefinitely. When I've saved up my passage money I shall go home. By then I shan't feel so awful over telling people what a gullible little fool I was, believing that a man loved me, when it wasn't love at all."

"You sound bitter, Maura. And I don't wonder. If only—"

"I'm not bitter, Paul. I'm not an ignorant little Irish girl any longer, that's all. And now, if we could finish up with a cup of coffee, I'd like to be going. I'm deathly tired."

This time she did not fall asleep in the car, had no dreams of a man's lips on hers. But when at last she was in bed in her attic room at *Mon Abri* she went straight into a deep sleep, scarcely stirring until cockcrow.

As so often, she arrived at the nursing home to find

things in something of a muddle, and to-day there was more confusion than ever.

Raymonde, who had been on duty for most of the previous day, had lost her temper with a difficult patient, who was now insisting on leaving and going home. And Gloria, the Night Sister, a well-trained, competent—and very charming—coloured girl, was threatening to hand in her notice over something that had happened during the night.

Her nursing orderlies were woefully inexperienced, and one of them had been responsible for a setback on the part of a patient.

Gloria had impressed on her the necessity of seeing that he had copious drinks of fruit-juice during the night, and had actually sent her to his room with a large jug of iced lime-juice. However, on the way something had distracted the girl—a call from another patient—and she had left the jug in the wrong room, where Gloria had found it in the early morning.

There had been a stormy interview between Mrs. Martin and Gloria, with Raymonde chipping in, and as a result the offender was given another chance. But Gloria, running into Maura, told her bitterly that the girl was useless, and was only being kept on because of the low pay she was receiving.

"You and I are the only fully trained nurses," she said. "The others, including Raymonde, are a set of ignoramuses. It's not because they can't get experienced nurses. It's because they won't pay them properly. As soon as I can find another job in Ste. Monique, I shall leave."

"I hope you won't." Maura looked dismayed. "When Hillside gets properly on its feet—"

"It won't, at this rate," Gloria declared. "And

another thing, I can't stand Raymonde. She has her favourites—undermines my authority—"

They heard someone coming, and Gloria went off, leaving Maura feeling very depressed and worried.

During the day matters mended. The irascible patient grudgingly accepted an apology from Maura, and the explanation that Raymonde had been overtired when she snapped at her. And the old gentleman who had been obliged to do without his jug of lime-juice was recovering from the ill effects of this neglect.

However, before she went home that evening Maura found herself in very grave trouble indeed.

She had now been at Hillside eight full weeks, and was due to receive her second month's salary.

On the previous occasion Mrs. Martin had actually sought her out to give her the money. And though Maura had to go to the office to-day and ask for it, since she was running very short, there seemed at first no difficulty.

Once again Mrs. Martin handed her an envelope containing, so she said, a cheque for the exact amount, but as Maura got up to go, she remarked with an embarrassed smile: "Sit down just a minute, while I explain something. Maybe you've noticed that I've had one or two very long-winded callers to-day."

Maura, mystified, returned that she had been too busy to pay much attention to anyone but her patients, and wondered what was coming.

Soon enough she knew.

"You'd better take a look at the cheque," Mrs. Martin told her, still more awkwardly. And she suddenly buried her face in her hands.

Tearing open the envelope, Maura at first noticed nothing wrong. The cheque seemed in perfect order. Then the date caught her eye, and she exclaimed in dismay: "It's post-dated. I can't use it for three weeks. And I'm cleaned right out!"

And into her mind swirled those warnings of Paul's which she had treated with such contempt.

Three weeks? Three months? Or never?

But Mrs. Martin had looked up now.

"You were paid well a month ago," she observed shortly. "Surely you must have something left."

"I explained to you when I came that I had arranged to pay Mrs. Perez in advance for my room," Maura retorted. "She gave me special terms."

Mrs. Martin looked scornful.

"That's her story. You'll have to keep her waiting, that's all. She's in no difficulties."

"I paid her yesterday when the money was due. I can hardly ask for it back. The few West Indian dollars I have won't get me far—so what do you expect me to do?"

Mrs. Martin considered. Then she said brusquely: "Give me back that post-dated cheque and I'll find you a few dollar bills to carry on with. In three weeks' time I'll give you another draft for what's owing to you." A pleading note came into her voice as she continued: "Surely you can manage that way, seeing what a jam I'm in!"

Maura was silent for a full minute. Then she asked: "If I agree, will you promise faithfully to settle up in full with me in three weeks' time? I don't want to clear out when you're in a difficulty, but if you can't pay me I shall have no alternative."

Gratitude shone in Mrs. Martin's eyes.

"You're a good soul, Maura," she said. "Just that little bit of time will make all the difference—give me a breathing-space." And then she went on, passing her hand over her tinted auburn hair: "It's the debts

I incurred when I started Hillside," she said. "I so wanted to give my patients the best of everything—build up a reputation for near-perfection. I'm absolutely certain the place can pay handsomely, if I'm given the chance. Meanwhile I'm harassed with bills. In England one could get credit from builders and tradespeople. Out here, it's pay up all the time. 'Pay up, or else—'"

Maura, not knowing how far she could believe her, but sorry for her all the same in her evident distress and anxiety, fumbled for words. But Mrs. Martin went on miserably: "Here's Gloria threatening to leave because I can only give her inexperienced assistants. But what can I do? She at least has always had her full salary, and on the dot. If she didn't, I'd have her father on the doorstep."

"She's not in nearly such an awkward position as I am," Maura pointed out ruefully. "Here am I, a stranger, thousands of miles from my family and friends. There's no one I can turn to."

"I'll keep my word to you," Mrs. Martin promised. "After all, you're just as valuable to me as Gloria. We'd have lost more than one patient to another nursing home just lately, but for your skill—and Irish charm." She paused, then continued appealingly: "I'm going to ask something of you, Maura—though I'm pretty sure that in your case it isn't necessary. You're too professional in your attitude, too loyal, to speak to anyone in this island of my difficulties."

Paul's warnings returned to her—and Geoffrey's well-meaning assurances. But pity for Mrs. Martin who, likeable or not, was staking all she had on this venture, made her give her promise. So long as she was just able to pay her way, she would say nothing to anyone about money troubles at the nursing home. And after a while things would surely work out.

And then, just as she was again getting up to go, Mrs. Martin said something else. Something which gave her a very unpleasant surprise.

"When I ask you not to talk to anyone in Ste. Monique about my financial problem," she observed with a strained smile, "I'm thinking of heedless gossip. If you could bring yourself to speak seriously to someone wealthy and influential, such as your friend and admirer, Paul Lasalle, you would be doing me a favour I could never repay."

"Paul Lasalle!" Maura exclaimed, thunderstruck.

"Well, yes, dear! He could set Hillside on its feet with a long-term loan and never miss the money. If you could explain to him—"

"But he's no friend of mine," Maura told her sharply. "I know him slightly, of course. But as it happens I don't even like him."

"I've heard very differently," Mrs. Martin said, and her tone was cold now. "In this little island you can't get away with much—even if it's only a gossiping servant that hears or sees you. In your case, the brother of a boy who used to work here, and who has a job in Clombières, saw you and Paul Lasalle kissing —in his car."

Maura's face flamed.

"I've never kissed Paul in my life," she said angrily. "And I never shall. Whenever we've met we've quarrelled. There's complete antipathy between us."

Mrs. Martin gave an incredulous smile, and shrugged her shoulders.

"Forget it," she said. "I'm sorry I asked you to help me. Good-night."

And turning to a pile of letters she indicated that the interview was at an end.

Maura's emotions, as she made her way back to *Mon Abri*, were in a turmoil.

What a crazy creature she had been, after all, to stay on in this little corner of the Caribbean, when she might have been back in London sharing a flat with Gwen, with a good salary, paid on the dot—and untroubled by foolish and lying gossip.

Why hadn't she treated Paul's natural wish to pay for her return voyage to England in a cool businesslike way? She could have insisted on regarding it as a loan and paid it back by instalments once she was home and in a good post.

She gave a groan. Why, oh, why had she landed herself in this fiendishly awkward situation?

Mrs. Martin's remark that she and Paul had been seen kissing in his car, out at Clombières, infuriated her, the more so as her flat denial obviously went for nothing.

It was all one of a piece.

Paul seeing her in company with Claude and taking it for granted that it was a pre-arranged meeting —even if he did not actually accuse her of trying to win his brother back from his former wife.

Some idler outside "The Three Fishers" spotting her with Paul and inventing this stupid story about seeing them kissing.

Just the kind of scandal that circulated in an obscure little island like Ste. Monique.

She fought down the memory of that strange and troubling—but not wholly unpleasant—delusion which had seized her at the end of that drive to Clombières—the notion that a man's lips had touched hers, that instant between waking and sleeping, in a light kiss. As though Paul would have kissed her when she was half asleep. Paul, who disliked and distrusted her.

And yet—that comment of Mrs. Martin's!

Ah, but it was easy to find another explanation for that piece of gossip.

"The Three Fishers" was a favourite haunt of Paul's. No doubt he and some other girl had been seen kissing in his car. No doubt there were many girls in Ste. Monique who liked to kiss—and be kissed by him.

A welcome distraction awaited her at the *pension*. Geoffrey Fanshawe, sitting on the veranda, a cool drink at his elbow, jumped up as she came down the path, and having fetched her a glass of lime-juice, invited her to come to a dance at the Country Club— a gala affair—on the following Saturday.

She had heard about this dance with a certain wistfulness at having no chance of going to it. For life at Ste. Monique had not brought her much gaiety and she loved to dance.

But on the verge of accepting she remembered Phyllis Reeves, and her laughing warning to her to keep off the grass where Geoffrey was concerned, and she asked seriously: "What about Phyllis?"

"She can't get out on a Saturday evening—at least, hardly ever," Geoffrey told her. "As you know, she's responsible for all the entertainments at the Florida-Carib, and it's full up at week-ends." And then he added, a shade impatiently: "In any case, we're just friends, Phyllis and I—not engaged, or anything like that."

That last remark cut no ice with Maura. She knew that, on Phyllis's side, at least, there were warmer feelings than friendship. However, if Phyl could not get off for the dance there was no reason why she herself should not go with Geoffrey.

So she accepted with pleasure and at once began, in true feminine fashion, considering which of the dresses she had worn on her outward journey would be most suited to this important occasion.

At work next day she learned that Raymonde was also going to this gala affair—with Alan Field, the doctor who had blamed her, soon after her arrival at the nursing home, for carelessness which, had he but known it, was entirely Raymonde's fault.

"Of course, if Gloria suddenly boils up again and clears out, one of us will have to stay on duty," Raymonde pointed out. "We can't both be out of the place if there's no qualified Night Sister."

Maura refrained from pointing out that Raymonde herself was singularly lacking in training and experience—but for once in a way Raymonde decided to make capital out of this.

"I'm afraid you would have to be the Cinderella," she said over-sweetly. "I couldn't take the responsibility."

But Maura was not impressed by this sudden show of humility.

"I have no intention of doing double duty," she said. "And for more than one reason."

Raymonde gave her a sharp glance, well aware of the little matter of Maura's salary. And Maura left her to her own reflections.

That evening, however, she unburdened herself to Gwen in a letter. She had told her, early on, of the revelation which had greeted her on first arriving in Ste. Monique of Claude's previous marriage and of his reconciliation with his former wife, and had kept up a desultory correspondence with her ever since.

Knowing Gwen so well from having shared a flat in London with her for more than two years, she could foresee pretty accurately what her friend would say about her present difficulty.

She would point out that if Mrs. Martin couldn't find the money to pay her nurses' salaries promptly and in full, she would be strongly tempted to let Maura be the first to go short—knowing her difficult position, isolated from family and friends, and a stranger in the island.

"Put your crazy Irish pride in your pocket," Gwen would say, "and tell Paul you will accept the offer of his family to pay your passage to England. Stop worrying what people here will think of your returning to London unmarried—and come home!"

She felt better after writing to Gwen. It was such a strain keeping one's problems and troubles to one's self. And she began looking forward to the dance, determined, whatever happened at the nursing home, to go to it.

Fortunately Gloria, who happened to prefer doing night duty to working during the day, had settled down to an uneasy truce with Mrs. Martin, so both Raymonde and Maura were free to attend the dance.

Geoffrey, in good spirits as usual, paid Maura some very pretty compliments on her crimson taffeta dress. He remembered her wearing it when dancing with her on the liner which brought them both out from England, and thinking how lovely she looked with her white skin and dark hair.

And he added under his breath, helping her cover her bare shoulders with her silvery stole: "If I hadn't, from the moment Gwen introduced us on the quay at Southampton, thought of you as an engaged girl—"

He didn't finish the sentence, and she was glad, for it bordered on disloyalty to Phyllis. Besides, though Geoffrey was a dear, she could not imagine ever falling for him, even if he were free as air.

They arrived—intentionally—at the Country Club a little late, Geoffrey declaring that it always took time for an affair like this to warm up.

But Maura could not even pretend to be bored or blasé, and gave a gasp of delight as he turned the car into the drive.

She had driven by the Club more than once during the day, but had never seen it by night lit up, as now, by fairy lights which gleamed not only from the long white house itself, but from the trees with which it was surrounded.

Moonlight, and the soft compulsive music of a steel band, added to the beauty of the scene. It was sheer fairyland.

They parked the car and went into the house to pay their respects to the Administrator and his wife—for it was a charity dance, run under their patronage.

Years ago when Sugar was King, and free labour was provided by slaves—Africans brought in chains from their homeland—the house had belonged to one of the French families who had fled from France at the time of the Revolution.

Evidently they had been gifted with good taste as well as money, for the large, lofty rooms were beautifully proportioned with delicately moulded ceilings and panelling which still bore traces of exquisitely painted scenes of island life.

Dancing had begun, though there were as yet only a few couples, and after cool drinks at one of the little tables on the veranda, Geoffrey and Maura went back into the ballroom.

At first she recognised nobody, but half an hour later Raymonde drifted in with Alan Field, and within a few minutes a party arrived which included Paul and—to her astonishment—Phyllis Reeves.

She and Geoffrey were sitting out in the grounds, chatting idly and watching the fireflies, and the newcomers went into the house without noticing them—a temporary respite for Maura, who had begun to feel sharply embarrassed.

However, if Geoffrey was ill at ease also—and she thought he certainly should be—he showed no sign of it.

"So Phyl was able to get away from the Florida-Carib after all!" he observed lightly. "Well, she and I have been dancing together quite a bit since we came to Ste. Monique and I daresay she'll be glad of a change of partner. I can't say I regret it myself," and he smiled across at her.

"You'll be able to cut in," Maura pointed out quickly. "I shan't mind sitting out a few dances."

"False modesty, my dear!" he told her cheerfully. "You're a knockout to-night, and you know it. You can't possibly have missed all the sheeps' eyes that have been cast in your direction. You'd be snapped up in a minute. Even your *bête noir* might have a try!"

But Maura was thoroughly put out.

"If you're referring to Paul Lasalle, nothing on earth would induce me to dance with him—nor would he ask me," she said haughtily. "Not if you left me alone for the rest of the evening."

"Which I'm certainly not doing, my sweet. But we're bound to run into his party, and exchange polite nothings with them. After all, this isn't a hotel, like the Florida-Carib. It's a club."

As it turned out there was no obvious opportunity for conversation with Paul's set until, just before supper, Maura encountered Phyllis in the cloakroom, fixing a spray of pink roses more securely into her blonde hair.

"Can I help you, Phyl?" Maura exclaimed, adding quickly: "I didn't expect to see you here. I thought you had to be on duty on Saturday nights."

"So took the opportunity of consoling Geoffrey!" The note of amusement in Phyllis's voice did not ring quite true.

There were other girls in the long room, and Maura lowered her own voice as she said evenly: "I wouldn't have accepted Geoffrey's invitation if I'd known you were free."

"Oh, don't worry! Paul seemed quite pleased to find me at a loose end when he drifted into the hotel early this evening." And then she added coldly, flicking a powder-puff over her pretty face: "I was with him, you know, when he suddenly caught sight of you with his brother. And I must say it shook me. I quite thought you'd done with Claude, now he'd patched up his marriage."

"So I have!"

"It didn't look like it—going off in a bus together."

Maura's eyes flashed.

"You and Paul aren't exactly overflowing with charity. It doesn't occur to you that I might have an honourable explanation."

"Oh, you've excellent reasons for everything," was Phyllis's retort to this, continuing, after a tiny pause: "I thought you were a decent kid, but I'm beginning to wonder if you're as ingenuous as I imagined."

Deeply hurt by this unexpected attack from someone whom she had looked upon as a friend, Maura said nothing but, her dark head held high, went back to the ballroom in search of Geoffrey.

He was waiting to take her in to supper and, to her dismay, led her to a big oval table where Paul and some of his guests were already seating themselves.

"Can't we have a table to ourselves, Geoffrey?" she demanded. She spoke softly, but there happened to be a lull in the conversation just then, and her words came out all too clearly in their Irish lilt—causing Paul, for one, to turn and look at her.

"I tried hard," Geoffrey murmured apologetically. "So did Dr. Field and Raymonde. But all the small tables were booked beforehand. The four of us have been put here."

More and more people arrived and soon every table had its quota, the Administrator and his wife sitting at the top of the room with some visiting V.I.P.s.

Phyllis, a picture in rose-pink, seated herself at Paul's right hand, and Maura found herself between Geoffrey and the elderly Dr. Craig, Alan Field's senior partner.

Dr. Craig had on his right an attractive middle-aged woman, and though Maura knew him only slightly, for he did not attend at the nursing home, he proved genial and friendly, and lost no time in introducing her to his other neighbour.

"Mrs. Lasalle, this is Maura O'Shea, a nurse at Hillside," he said pleasantly. "If you have already met you must forgive my officiousness."

"I've heard of you, Miss O'Shea, and I'm very glad to make your acquaintance now," Mrs. Lasalle said, smiling, and speaking in a voice so gentle, it was as though a soothing hand were laid on Maura's sore heart. "My mother was half Irish and used to show us some lovely sketches her grandmother had made. We must have a talk about Ireland some time."

"That's very kind of you." Maura's tone was noncommittal.

But Mrs. Lasalle did not take the hint and drop the subject.

"We must fix a definite date for you to come to tea," she said. "And afterwards I must show you my garden."

She turned away then to speak to her other neighbour—it had been awkward talking across Dr. Craig—and seeing Geoffrey occupied with Raymonde, Maura chatted for a little with Dr. Craig.

Many times she was conscious that Paul was looking at her, particularly when Geoffrey engaged her in conversation again. But she was careful to avoid his eyes. Was he obtuse enough to imagine that she intended to accept his stepmother's invitation? She could hardly believe it.

She managed after supper to avoid Paul's party, but dancing brought her in contact with Paul again. He cut in and swept her off in a quickstep almost before she realised what was happening.

As she knew already, he was a first-rate dancer—even better than Geoffrey—and had she disliked him less she would have delighted to have him as a partner. As it was she wished with all her heart that he had left her alone.

Or was that really so? Didn't she, all against her will, experience something of that thrill she had felt months and months ago in London when she had first met him?

In those early days she had thought far more of him than of Claude, and perhaps if it had been he and not his brother who had stayed on in London—!

But in those days she had known him as little as she had known Claude. Reflecting on the way he had come to her help when she had been knocked down by that thief, the gentleness with which he had lifted her out of the gutter, the concern he had shown for her, she had had no conception how differently he could behave when angered. How hard and distrustful he could be, how lacking in charity.

They exchanged not a word at first, but when he saw another couple approaching, and guessed that he would soon be losing his partner, he said with something like distaste: "Maura, do you have to play up to Fanshawe in such an obvious way? Can't you leave him and Phyllis alone?"

This further injustice was too much for Maura.

"Don't worry," she exclaimed under her breath. "I shall leave this gossip-ridden little island the moment I can."

And breaking away from him, she went over and sat by someone who, surely, she could not be accused of trying to allure—Dr. Craig.

At first, in spite of the elderly doctor's friendliness, Maura found conversation difficult. She had looked forward to this dance at the Country Club as a break in the monotony of her life in Ste. Monique. And everything had gone wrong.

There was Phyllis, implying that she was hankering after Claude, and in the same breath suggesting that she was setting her cap at Geoffrey—the man whom Phyllis regarded as her special property. And as if that wasn't enough—Paul was accusing her of disloyalty to her friend.

Friend!

She hadn't one real friend in the island, and for the first time in her life she realised to the full what it meant to be quite desperately lonely.

However, from sheer good manners, she tried hard to respond to Dr. Craig's attempts to draw her out, and gradually succeeded in regaining the appearance, at least, of composure.

Before long Dr. Craig began talking about the nursing home.

"I've heard rather varying accounts of it," he said, "and perhaps I shouldn't be discussing it with you. But it all boils down to what is common knowledge— the lack of fully-trained nurses."

"There's a shortage of staff everywhere," she said, wondering where this conversation was leading. "In England—well, what we'd do without nurses from the West Indies I can't imagine."

He nodded absently, then went on: "As you know, I have almost nothing to do with Hillside. I leave it to my partner to attend there. But I happened to hear that you had recent experience at one of the big London hospitals in the care of children—and this evening I took a little girl there, a child in whom I have a particular interest."

"Unless you arrange it with Mrs. Martin she might not be under my care," Maura pointed out.

"I particularly asked that you should nurse Stella," was his quiet response. "And if you'll forgive my talking shop I can explain why, instead of waiting to contact you at Hillside to-morrow."

He paused, then asked, in the same steady tone: "Did you happen to hear newsboys shouting this evening—or see anything on the screen—about an attempted murder on the other side of the island?"

She shook her head and exclaimed in horror: "The attempted murder of a child?"

"No. As you'll read to-morrow in the papers, the wife of a South American businessman was sleeping alone last night in their bungalow, alone except for a little girl of five, her husband having been obliged to fly to the mainland for some conference or other. A gardener, who had been discharged for theft, broke in during the night and tried to rifle the jewel safe in her bedroom. Maybe he thought she was away, too. Anyway when she switched on the light he attacked her with a machete. She screamed, and Stella woke up and started screaming too—"

"The woman—was she badly hurt?" Maura exclaimed.

"She'll recover, but it will be a long job. She's in hospital in Belleray. I took Stella to Hillside, partly because the air is so much better out there and partly because I remembered Paul Lasalle mentioning not long ago your experience with children."

Too confused to think clearly, Maura asked: "How did they know the identity of the woman's assailant?"

"Because the little girl kept calling out even on the car ride to Hillside: 'Manoel, *don't*!'"

"I hope Hillside is the right place for her," Maura said uncertainly.

"With you to look after her—yes! Mrs. Martin was most sympathetic to the idea of your taking her on as a private patient, especially as I was able to find a retired S.R.N. to carry on your ordinary duties. Money is no object with these South Americans, and the child's father approves. He arrived back this afternoon, staying at the Florida-Carib."

"She'll be all right to-night. There's a fully-trained nurse on duty."

He nodded.

"The child is having sedation, of course. She should sleep without stirring. And to-morrow morning you'll be there to take over."

"I'll certainly do my best," Maura told him. "But I'm rather surprised at your asking me to do anything so important—and difficult. Your partner, Dr. Field, doesn't think much of me."

Dr. Craig smiled.

"He does, actually! Admires the professional way in which you accepted blame for someone else's fault. A little matter of bed-sores!"

Maura flushed.

"How did he find out?"

"I believe the offender confessed—and did herself a bit of good with him. It couldn't have been easy."

Maura was silent for a full minute. Then she said jerkily: "Life is very odd—and so are human beings."

His smile deepened.

"Are you only just discovering that?"

"Well, it's very queer. People you think are your friends turn on you. And others, who apparently dislike you, do you a kindness."

"I don't know that it was exactly a kindness on Miss Sorel's part to own up to Dr. Field that he'd blamed you wrongly. We all have consciences, even if they're not always in working order."

Maura said nothing. She had been thinking less of Raymonde than of Paul. How was it that he could treat her in such an inconsistent fashion—accusing her at one moment, if not in so many words, of being a man-hunter, and at the next stressing her excellence as a nurse? It hardly made sense.

Geoffrey came up just then to claim her, but he was not allowed to monopolise her for the rest of the evening. While they were sitting out on the veranda other dancers joined them and there was a general shuffle. It gave her the chance of meeting people whom hitherto she had only known by sight; of losing that sense of moving within a small constricting circle.

Paul and Phyllis, too, were dancing with different partners, and once, to her sharp relief, she saw Geoffrey go up to Phyllis and ask her for a dance. But her satisfaction was short-lived. It was evident that Phyllis had turned him down, for he moved away, looking thoroughly annoyed.

The only member of Paul's party with whom she came in direct contact again was Mrs. Lasalle, who singled her out at the end of the evening, when they were all fetching their wraps from the cloakroom, to repeat her invitation.

Once more Maura gave a polite but evasive reply, and finally, seeing that the older woman looked a little hurt, she murmured, flushed and embarrassed, that there were strong reasons why she could not come up to tea with her.

"I understand, my dear—more than you realise, perhaps." Mrs. Lasalle had a singularly sweet smile. "So I'll just say this. If you are ever in want of a friend, get in touch with me. We might find much to say to each other."

Coming on that desolating sense of loneliness this remark warmed Maura's heart. Had Mrs. Lasalle not stood in that close relation to Paul and Claude she would certainly have responded to her kindly gesture. As it was, the very thought of going to the Lasalle home made her shrink into herself with embarrassment. Surely if Mrs. Lasalle knew the whole story she would not expect her to come?

She found Geoffrey in a strange mood, as they drove home to *Mon Abri*. A mood of exhilaration that didn't ring true.

He had enjoyed the dance immensely, largely because of having been blessed with such an attractive partner.

"Apart from dancing like a fairy, you're so sweet, Maura," he told her. "All the men were envying me —asking if a romance was blowing up between us, and all that."

"I hope you gave them a firm, 'No!'" Maura returned quickly.

"Not a bit of it. I treated them to a smoke-screen. And why not?"

"Because that sort of nonsense will ruin your friendship with Phyllis. She's already annoyed with me."

"And with me! And if she thinks that's the way to hold a man, she's right off the track. Jealousy is a very ugly emotion!"

"But a very human one. Have you never suffered from it?"

"Maybe. But I've never made a fool of myself by showing it—the way Phyllis did to-night."

Maura did not answer for a moment. Then she said seriously: "I'd rather a person had a quick temper than a smouldering one. And don't forget, people coming to work in the tropics are apt to get tired and edgy—until they become used to the climate. I do, I know."

"My dear, you've had enough to spoil your temper—with Claude bringing you out here to marry you—and then decamping to his ex-wife."

Again she hesitated, observing at last: "I suppose I shall always bear scars. But if they pain a little sometimes, as scars are apt to do, the hurt will only be to my pride. You see, my love for Claude—if, indeed, it was real love—didn't die a lingering death. He killed it stone dead by his deception."

"I can well understand that. You're a great girl, Maura. Phyl's always talking about your courage. She likes you a lot, Maura."

"She did until to-night. And I hope she will again. But I rather think that's up to you, Geoffrey."

He gave a little laugh.

"If you weren't so remarkably attractive, my dear, with your looks and your Irish lilt, it would be easier to convince her, and a few other silly people, that you're no vamp."

She felt like flaring up—for the mean and hurtful suggestion that she was deliberately setting out to fascinate the men she met was becoming far too frequent. But she controlled herself, and as they turned in at the gate of *Mon Abri*, said coolly: "Please try. And thanks for a very pleasant evening."

Next morning she awoke to thoughts of the little girl who was to be her patient, and with these came the memory that it was through Paul's recommendation that Dr. Craig had entrusted Stella to her.

She thrust it aside. All that mattered was to do her best for the poor mite who had undergone this terrible experience. Nothing else counted—not even her professional reputation.

Mrs. Martin, too, was deeply concerned over the child. Maura had never seen her so moved.

At any other time she would have been full of jubilation that at last Dr. Craig had deigned to send one of his own private patients to Hillside, but this consideration now took a back place. She had no jealousy that Maura had been singled out to look after Stella. She was relieved that she had so well-trained a nurse available, and thankful to have found a substitute for Maura in the shape of the elderly S.R.N., Sister Baker, whom Dr. Craig had recommended to her.

Maura, taking over from the Night Sister, went straight to Stella's room.

She was a pretty child, with black curly hair and enormous dark eyes that looked up drowsily as Maura entered, so expressionless as to make clear that she was still under the influence of the drug which had been given her.

Mrs. Martin who had joined Maura repeated the simple directions which Dr. Craig had given her the previous evening, and telling her that the doctor expected to be there soon after ten, with the child's father, left her to her patient.

She tidied the room, brought in a jug of iced fruit juice and a vase of bright-coloured flowers, and then, as the child gradually shed her sleepy looks, fetched her some milk and cornflakes.

For a few moments Stella ate what was given her, though too languid to use the spoon herself. And then suddenly she pushed the bowl away and looking up at Maura asked her in a shrill, shaking voice: "Why did Manoel hit Mama with his machete?"

"Because he was a very wicked man," Maura told her gently. "But your mama is all right now—"

"She fell on the floor," Stella whimpered. "And Manoel ran away. Her eyes were shut like she was asleep, and she wouldn't wake up when I called her."

"He hurt her badly, but she's getting better now. She's in hospital where they know how to make her quite well. Your daddy's seeing her this morning, and then he's coming on to see you."

"I want to see Mama!" A large tear trickled down Stella's round, pale face.

"So you shall when you're quite well, too. If you eat up your breakfast, Daddy will be very pleased—so let's try again."

It needed a little coaxing to get her to take a few more spoonfuls of cereal: a small, sweet banana went down more easily. Then came the business of bathing her under the shower, and combing out her long black ringlets.

Deft but gentle in all her movements, Maura found herself gaining the child's confidence.

"You're like Mummy, you don't tug," Stella said. "And you don't get soap in my eyes, either."

"That's because I'm used to looking after children when they aren't very well," Maura told her. "I used to nurse in a hospital where there were lots and lots of them. A long way from here, it was: in London."

"Were some of them naughty?"

Maura searched her memory for anecdotes.

"There was a little boy called Tommy," she began—and sailed off on a story of a small boy who was always getting out of bed the moment the nurse's back was turned, and trying to hide the other children's toys.

"I wouldn't have liked him to hide my Teddy," Stella declared, and then she asked anxiously, looking up into Maura's face: "My daddy will bring Teddy, won't he? He'd be dreadfully lonely without me. And if Manoel went back he'd—he'd die of fright."

Maura, who had taken her on her knee to comb her hair, cuddled her up to her.

"Don't worry any more about Manoel, pet. He's locked up at the police station."

"Until he's sorry, I s'pose!"

"That's just about it. Anyway he can't hurt or frighten Teddy or anyone else. So don't fret about it."

The little girl was very tired now, and Maura popped her back into bed. She lay there quietly, holding Maura's hand tightly, but when she dozed off the same words, in an accent of terror, rose to her lips: "Manoel, *don't*!"

She woke up just before her father's visit, and her joy and relief at seeing him—carrying Teddy, moreover—were infinitely touching.

"I know all about Mama," she announced, when the first hugging and kissing were over. "She's in hospital where people know *ezackly* how to make her better soon."

Mr. Gonzalez, a dark, good-looking man in his early thirties, flashed Maura a grateful smile.

"She's in a nice little room, something like this, and has a kind nurse, all to herself, just as you have."

"Does she tell her stories? My nurse has some lovely true ones."

"Maybe she will later on. At present Mama is sleeping a lot. When she stays awake longer you'll be able to go and see her."

The child's face puckered.

"Can't I go and see her to-day?"

Dr. Craig, who had driven Mr. Gonzalez over, came in just then.

"You must have some more sleep yourself, young lady, before you're fit to go out in a car. But I'll tell you what. Listen to those stories Nurse tells you— she's lots more, I know, some of them about Ireland —and save them up to tell Mummy when you see her."

He drew Maura out of the room then, leaving father and small daughter together, and told her that

Mrs. Gonzalez, though badly injured, was out of danger.

"She came very near losing her arm," he said, "and if neighbours hadn't heard screams, she'd have died from loss of blood. We gave her a transfusion within minutes of getting her to hospital, and she's more than holding her own."

And then he went on to make some inquiries about Stella, and to issue further directions about her treatment.

"The way she's handled for the next week or two is going to make all the difference later on," he said. "More than anything she wants mothering. And that's what she'll be getting from you, I know. Care, common sense—and love."

He turned back into the room, but stopped to speak to her again.

"I shall tell Paul Lasalle," he said, "that he couldn't have suggested a more suitable nurse for a child in Stella's state."

Maura's eyes widened.

"I thought he spoke of me in general terms, in connection with my training."

The old doctor gave her a keen, faintly humorous glance from beneath his shaggy eyebrows.

"Is it all that important?" he said.

Within a fortnight—sooner than anyone had dared to hope—Stella was sleeping naturally and eating normally. She no longer needed medical attention. But she still woke up, from time to time in a nightmare, and Dr. Craig, while agreeing with Maura that a nursing home was no place for a child up and about and running around, warned Mr. Gonzalez that motherly care and watchful affection were still essential for his small daughter if she was not to suffer in later years from memories of that terrible night.

But where was he to find this care? poor harassed Mr. Gonzalez demanded. He himself was up to the eyes in business activities, all his scanty leisure being spent at the hospital. His wife would not be fit to return home for at least a month—and then only as a convalescent. And though his one unmarried sister —Stella's favourite aunt—would be able to come to the rescue eventually she was tied up with her job in Buenos Aires for several weeks.

It was young Stella herself who pointed to a solution of the problem—and in no uncertain manner.

She would be a good girl and go wherever Daddy said so long as Sister went with her, and she could see "poor Mama" very, very often.

Her father tried to explain that trained nurses only looked after children when they were ill—that he would have to look out for a nice nanny for her. But this suggestion upset Stella so much that he had, perforce, to throw himself on Maura's kindness.

He was already staying at the Florida-Carib, and would be immensely grateful if she would bring Stella to the hotel and stay there, looking after her, for a month.

He would pay her a higher salary than she ordinarily received at Hillside—a remark which caused Maura ironical amusement—and make it worth while to Mrs. Martin to release her for that period.

Maura hesitated over the proposition, but a brief conversation with Mrs. Martin decided her to accept it—looking upon it less as a job than as a paid holiday.

Even in this short time her heart had warmed to Stella—to her small clinging arms, her soft childish kisses. And apart from that she gathered that Mr. Gonzalez' generosity would help her worried employer tide over one of the many financial crises that threatened her.

"But what I really need," Mrs. Martin said wearily, "is an injection of capital—a few thousand dollars. I'm afraid I went to the lengths of sounding Mr. Gonzalez on the subject, but he shied off it at once. Said he never had much in the way of loose assets lying around."

Maura could only look—and feel—sympathetic, and after a moment Mrs. Martin continued, touching her beautifully waved and tinted hair in a distracted way: "I hinted at the distress and anxiety I felt over getting behindhand with salaries. But his pity was all for my nurses, not for me. He singled you out, rather naturally, and couldn't understand how such a splendid young nurse could tolerate working in a small nursing home on a tiny island, unless there was a man in the case."

Maura went crimson, and Mrs. Martin who had been watching her closely, observed with an irritatingly sweet smile: "I told him you were something of a man's girl by all accounts, but that I really knew nothing of your private affairs."

Trying hard to recover her composure, and keep her temper, Maura made no comment on this impertinent remark.

She merely inquired whether Mr. Gonzalez would wish her to wear uniform, and at what time he would be calling to drive her and Stella to the hotel.

But those words of Mr. Gonzalez, repeated to her by Mrs. Martin, stuck in her mind like a barb.

"Unless there was a man in the case!"

Could it be—could it possibly be—that down in her

subconscious mind there lay her true motive, shaming, unacknowledged, for staying on in Ste. Monique?

Was it simply pride that kept her from accepting the money from Paul for her return passage to England—even as a loan? Could it be that under all her indignation with him, her sense of his injustice, there was the stronger, far fiercer feeling, that to move forever out of his orbit, to part with him finally and forever, would be utterly unbearable?

She did her best to tear this wounding thought from her mind. Could there be worse humiliation than to love a man who openly despised and distrusted her—who lost no opportunity of urging her to leave the Caribbean and go home to England, where she belonged? Compared with this, Claude's disgraceful treatment of her counted for nothing, simply because she had for long regarded him with complete indifference, wondering, if she thought of him at all, what she had seen in him but superficial charm.

The prospect of staying at the Florida-Carib gave her mixed sensations.

She was certain to run into Paul during her month there, for he used the hotel almost as a club. And though she longed for even the briefest encounter with him, she dreaded it with almost equal intensity.

There was Phyllis Reeves, too, whom she was bound to meet whenever she had to call at the office—Phyllis who had once, believing in her, befriended her in her greatest need but who now thought her false and dishonourable—utterly ungrateful. Would she ever be able to put things right with her?

She had decided to give up her little attic room at *Mon Abri* altogether instead of paying Mrs. Perez a retaining fee.

Geoffrey had protested energetically over this, declaring that she would never find such cheap and satisfactory accommodation again in the whole of Ste. Monique, and adding that although she now refused all his invitations, he would miss her intolerably. The house would be a morgue without her.

He was right, she knew, about the difficulty of finding another room, but she hoped her move would count for something with Phyllis, show her once and for all that she had no designs on Geoffrey—and also it would help her to add to her precious but most meagre savings. For there was clearly no stability in her job at Hillside, and in spite of what people said about the shortage of nurses she might not find another suitable one immediately.

To her relief Phyllis Reeves was off duty when Mr. Gonzalez brought her and Stella to the hotel. Nor did anyone appear to remember the broken girl who had stayed one night there—and left precipitately—many weeks ago.

Mr. Gonzalez had booked a room for herself and Stella on the floor above his own: a quiet spacious room at the back of the hotel where, if the child awoke in a nightmare, screaming, she would be unlikely to disturb other guests.

Compared with her attic at *Mon Abri* it was sheerest luxury, and she and Stella were soon making themselves at home, "Teddy" being tucked up firmly in his young mistress's bed, and ordered to be a good boy and go to sleep.

A great vase of coral-coloured *ixora* blossom stood in a corner, and Stella, running to look at it, declared gaily that "Daddy" must have had it put there. But there was a note attached to one of the stems, addressed to Maura in a fairly familiar handwriting, and when she tore the little envelope open she found a message from Geoffrey.

"A few flowers to welcome you and make you feel at home in that barracks of a place. I am going to miss you horribly at *Mon Abri*, even though you let me see so little of you."

She frowned as she read it. Could Geoffrey have been more tactless? Almost certainly Phyllis would know about these flowers—and feel more bitter than ever towards her.

The lift was just a few yards along the corridor, and as soon as she and Stella were tidy they went down to Mr. Gonzalez' private sitting-room where a smiling young waiter was setting out a simple meal for the little girl.

"Mr. Gonzalez say Missy eat at six o'clock," he told Maura, "and you have dinner downstairs with him at the usual time—eight-thirty."

"Does that suit you, Nurse?" Mr. Gonzalez had just come in from the adjoining bedroom.

"I'm afraid it doesn't," Maura returned pleasantly but firmly. "I'd like my dinner sent up to my bedroom on a tray."

"That's disappointing. I thought I was going to have a charming companion for meals." Mr. Gonzalez looked slightly put out. "I'd already arranged with one of the chambermaids to keep an eye on Stella while you were downstairs."

"Maura promised she wouldn't leave me and Teddy alone!" Stella's tone was shrill, and her face had begun to pucker.

"That's all right, darling." Maura's protective arm went round her, as she dropped on her knees beside her. And then she looked up at the child's father, smiling in a way that any man would have surely found irresistible.

"For all other meals you'll have two charming companions," she pointed out to him. "At least we hope you'll find us that, don't we, Stella?"

"There'll be three charming 'panions for you, Daddy." Stella's expression was happy again. "Teddy will prob'ly come if he's not too busy."

"Very kind of him," her father returned with grave politeness, and he told the young waiter: "Bring Miss O'Shea the menu and wine list. And see she has the best of everything."

A letter stood propped against a wine-glass on her dinner-tray that night and the waiter told her, apologetically, that she should have had it before. The gentleman who had brought the flowers had dropped it in at the same time.

It was an air letter, addressed to her at *Mon Abri*, and she took it up eagerly, hungry as always for news from home, and seeing at once that her correspondent was Gwen, writing from the London flat.

> "I've wonderful news," Gwen wrote. "My cousins in Raballo have put me in the way of securing an excellent job in one of the best hospitals there. There is a vacancy for another S.R.N. too, and I have told them you'll almost certainly want to try for it. They'll be needing help in a couple of months' time, which will make it a rush for me, unless I fly out. I enclose an application form and hope you will get it off to the address given on it as soon as you possibly can. What fun it will be to work together again.
>
> "Very much love.
>
> > "Gwen."

The delicious meal on her tray cooled as she sat there in a torment of indecision.

An opening like this, coming just at this moment, seemed like an answer to prayer. And yet—to leave Ste. Monique for good, knowing that in all probability she would never meet Paul again—!

Presently she began to toy with her food—the spicy chicken dish, with its varied vegetable accompaniment of egg-plant, sweet potatoes, chick-peas and plantain, the sweet juicy fruit and many-coloured ice-cream—but could work up very little appetite. And presently she pushed the tray aside and went to lean out of the window to catch the light breeze.

The outlook from the back was less attractive than from the front where, as she remembered, one gazed straight out on to the sea. But it was lovely enough, when, as now, the moonlight silvered the garden, and the tree-bordered road beyond. Even here the fireflies danced and from the near-distance came the sound which all her life she would, she felt sure, associate with the Caribbean—the insistent piping of a myriad bull-frogs.

What should she do? What did she really want to do?

And then, as this question throbbed in her brain, the answer suddenly came.

Down in the moonlit garden a man and a woman were strolling, and as a ray lit them up she recognised Phyllis and Paul, both in evening dress. They were in close conversation, and as she watched them, utterly unable to take her eyes from them, Phyllis moved into Paul's arms, and they kissed.

CHAPTER 5

THAT little scene in the moonlit garden came to Maura as a direct answer to a question.

Ever since the Gala Night at the Country Club, when Paul had brought Phyllis along as his partner, she had wondered whether their evident liking for each other would develop into a warmer feeling.

Unreasonable as it was to be hurt by the visible proof that they had indeed fallen in love—for what had Paul ever shown her but dislike and distrust?—she felt utterly stricken, realising fully, at last, how deeply she cared for him.

Instinct had told her, at their very first meeting, that he was the man she wanted to marry, but she had smothered the idea as romantic nonsense. Irish girls had their heads screwed on better than that. They didn't fall for men without strong encouragement. And so she had put him out of her head, and Claude, the man on the spot, who had set out to win her heart, talked of love and marriage, had taken his place.

Useless to tell herself that in those early days Paul had not been drawn to her as she to him. She knew now, with a knowledge that came from the heart rather than the head, that she might have come out to the Caribbean engaged to him, not to Claude, had she followed that first intuition.

"There is a tide in the affairs of men"—the Shakespearean quotation, learned at school, slid into her mind. She had missed the tide, and must pay the penalty.

At least she knew now what she must do—say a firm good-bye to Ste. Monique and fall in with Gwen's timely suggestion that they should take up work in a leading hospital in Raballo. Eight hundred miles was a considerable distance, even in the Caribbean where so much travel was done by plane.

Nursing with Gwen, who was almost like a sister to her, she would start life afresh, burying sad memories so deep that like noxious weeds they would never spring up again to hurt her.

She had intended to try to reach an understanding with Phyllis over her own friendship with Geoffrey— a one-sided friendship since she had done nothing to encourage it—but now decided to let things alone. Phyllis, absorbed with Paul, would hardly wish to discuss Geoffrey's defection.

In any case she was soon to discover that Phyllis intended to treat her with the impersonal courtesy she showed to other guests. If she needed anything for herself or for her little charge, she had only to go to the office and mention it to Phyllis, and her wish would be attended to, politely if not with a smile.

The only guests with whom she mixed were mothers with small children, and this was more on Stella's account than her own. The child needed playmates— to have them was part of her cure—and Maura, seeing her splashing happily in the children's swimming pool, felt deep satisfaction. She was a different child from the white-faced little girl who had been put in her care so short a time ago.

Geoffrey still wrote and telephoned to her, with invitations to spend her free time with him, and now she no longer gave him automatic refusals. She had already made it clear to him that she could never look upon him as anything but a friend, and this being so, there seemed no reason, in view of Phyllis's indifference, why she should not go for an occasional drive or picnic with him at week-ends, when Mr. Gonzalez was at leisure to look after his small daughter.

Paul she seldom saw, and when she did meet him they found little to say to each other, Stella's presence giving them an excellent excuse.

Embarrassingly, however, Stella decided that after "Daddy" and Dr. Craig, Mr. Lasalle was the nicest man she knew, and if she caught sight of him in the distance could hardly be restrained from rushing up to him.

"Don't you like him, Maura?" she would inquire in puzzled tones—she had soon dropped calling Maura by anything but her Christian name—and the reply: "That's not the point. He's a very busy man and we mustn't worry him" didn't really satisfy her.

The child's mother was making slow but steady progress, and Maura, taking Stella to visit her in hospital, found her very likeable—and deeply grateful for all she was doing for the little girl. And one afternoon, when the child had gone off with a Sister to take some toys to the children's ward, she said something that did much to soothe Maura's bitterness of heart.

"You know how people talk in these little islands!" she said, slipping her thin hand into Maura's. "I'd heard rumours that the new Irish nurse at Hillside was a bit of a vamp, and it worried me a little to hear that you were living at the Florida-Carib with Stella, in such close proximity to my husband. He's a dear, and I love and trust him. Still, men with Latin blood aren't quite as cold and detached as the English and Irish, and I was a tiny bit frightened. But the moment I saw you I knew that you were good all through."

"It would be rather a horrible woman who would take advantage of a woman in your position," Maura said, wide-eyed at the very idea, and she added, smiling: "You're right to trust me. And Latin or not, you can trust your husband, too. You're lucky, Mrs. Gonzalez, to have a man who's a charmer, but who loves you to adoration."

Mrs. Gonzalez squeezed her hand.

"I wish you the same luck, too. You deserve it." Continuing hesitantly: "This young man my husband mentions as a friend of yours, Geoffrey Fanshawe— does he mean anything to you? Or shouldn't I ask?"

"He's a friend, but nothing more," Maura told her quickly.

"If he has the right qualities love may come," Mrs. Gonzalez returned seriously. "Don't turn down a good man too readily. I nearly lost Carlos that way—sighing after a film star." She smiled faintly. "I thought Carlos dull and ordinary—only just discovered in time that he was, as you say, quite special."

Maura managed to echo her smile, but said nothing. She also had given her heart to someone quite special—but too late. He didn't want it.

She took time off that evening, Mr. Gonzalez being around, to go up to Hillside to fetch some clean laundry, and found Mrs. Martin in excellent spirits.

She took her into her little office, made her sit down, and from a corner cupboard produced a bottle of rum and two little bottles of ginger ale.

"I want you to join me in a celebration," she said, beaming at Maura. "Hillside is out of the rough at last. The Lasalle Company is lending me the capital

I so sorely need, and at a very low rate of interest. There will be no more delays in the payment of salaries. And yours, at least, will be raised."

"The Lasalle Company?" Maura's face took on a guarded expression.

"That's what I said." Mrs. Martin's smile had deepened. "Raymonde imagines"—she lowered her voice—"that Paul Lasalle is doing it on her account. She and Dr. Field went up to dinner with him and his mother one night, and she came home very pleased with herself. But I know better."

Maura said nothing, and Mrs. Martin went on gaily: "It's on your account, my dear. And though I oughtn't to tell you, I don't see why I shouldn't—in confidence, of course."

It was beyond Maura to refuse to listen to this disclosure, and Mrs. Martin told her triumphantly: "He insisted that I raised your salary by fifty per cent. I explained that you were already receiving more than any member of my staff—while admitting that there were sometimes delays in payment—but he was adamant."

Maura flushed, certain that Paul's motive was to furnish her with funds so that she could go home to England with all possible speed, ridding the island of her unwelcome presence.

She said coolly: "It's embarrassing for me; and I should have thought quite exasperating for you. Why should you be blackmailed into over-paying me?"

"That's nonsense, Maura. You're worth the increase, as you must be well aware. As for my personal reaction, acquiring the capital is all I care about. That you should get something out of the deal is only fair."

"What if I refuse to take it?" Maura exclaimed sharply.

"Then you'll be a fool!" was Mrs. Martin's retort. "Paul wouldn't withdraw the capital—things have gone too far for that—but it would be a most ungracious act on your part, and make things very awkward for me. He didn't want me to tell you. But that's like him—all for justice. If an English S.R.N. whom he happens to know isn't getting the salary she would be receiving in Britain—well, something must be done about it."

"How did he know what my salary was, anyway?" Maura demanded—wholly unconvinced by this explanation.

"Naturally he had access to all my books—and to be frank, he strongly advised other increases of pay. It was only yours on which he was insistent. And I had to admit that you were by far the best-trained nurse I had."

Maura finished the long, cool drink, and stood up.

"I'm glad your difficulties are solved, anyway," she said, trying not to sound too stiff. "I must pick up my clean laundry now, and get along."

Mrs. Martin flicked over the pages of her workmanlike engagement diary.

"You're due to return here in ten days' time, I see. I shall be glad to have you back. Sister Baker, the S.R.N. Dr. Craig found for us, is good, but a bit old for working so hard."

Maura acquiesced. Mr. Gonzalez would not need her much longer. Stella's favourite aunt was coming over from the Argentine to open up the house again, and her mother would be able to go there for her convalescence, with a competent staff to wait on her. How easy life could be for wealthy people in the

Caribbean—but how terrifying too. So long as they lived Mrs. Gonzalez and her little girl would be plagued, on and off, with memories of that night of stark horror.

She decided that, as she was in this direction, she would stroll along to *Mon Abri*. Mrs. Perez was erratic over forwarding letters and there might be something for her.

Before she reached the house Geoffrey overtook her in his car and gave her a lift for the rest of the way, telling her that she looked a dream in her pale blue linen dress.

"What shall we do this evening, Maura?" he asked cheekily.

"I wasn't aware that we were doing anything—together!"

"But I've been cherishing strong hopes that we might. I was going to ring you at the Florida-Carib as soon as I reached the *pension*. And now, here you are."

She hesitated.

Mr. Gonzalez had urged her that very day to take the opportunity of going out with her friends when, as now, he was able to take Stella over for a few hours.

And with Phyllis no longer interested in Geoffrey—!

He saw by her expression that he had won the day.

"We'll go dancing again at the Country Club," he said.

She picked up one or two letters from home and exchanged a few genial remarks with Mrs. Perez, who assured her that she missed her and would always find a corner for her at *Mon Abri* if she wanted to come back. And then Geoffrey ran her back to the Florida-Carib to arrange things with Mr. Gonzalez, and to change. He would be calling for her in a couple of hours' time.

Mr. Gonzalez was delighted that this chance of a pleasant evening had blown up. He and Stella both wanted to see her in all her finery before she left, and though she had nothing new to wear the white sharkskin, with its off-the-shoulder line, suited her as well as anything in her limited wardrobe.

Her audience could hardly have been more appreciative, and when it was time to go down to the ground floor lounge, Mr. Gonzalez insisted on accompanying her, and on buying for her at the little "shop," a tiny flask of expensive French perfume.

She had looked round for Geoffrey, but he had not yet arrived, and now she saw that Paul, sitting at a small table, ostensibly reading the evening paper, had been a witness of Mr. Gonzalez' generosity.

There was no reason why her employer should not give her a present from the hotel shop, even though prices there were fabulous, and most of the customers American tourists, their wallets stuffed with dollars. But at that moment—and a few minutes later when Geoffrey appeared, carrying a corsage for her—she would have preferred him to be far away.

However she retained her poise, said good-bye prettily to Mr. Gonzalez, and went off with Geoffrey, finding no necessity to take any notice of Paul who, anyway, had buried himself behind his newspaper.

Geoffrey, who was in almost unnaturally high spirits, lost no time in whisking her out of the hotel and into his car.

"Why did I ever think I liked Phyllis so much?" he exclaimed, as soon as they were out on the road and heading for the Country Club. "I caught sight of her standing outside her office just now, and gave her a smile and a wave. And what do you think? She cut me dead."

"Maybe she didn't see you," Maura said, beginning to feel a little uncomfortable.

"Of course she did. But she's a jealous little cat, that one—a cat in the manger, you might say. Thrilled to bits over her conquest of Paul Lasalle, but can't bear it if her former boy-friends take up with anyone else."

"What makes you think Paul is keen on her?" Maura asked him very casually, with no intention of telling Geoffrey that she had seen him kissing Phyllis.

He shrugged his shoulders.

"Oh, I don't know. People are talking. And you know how it is—no smoke without fire. Besides," and his voice hardened, "I've seen the way she looks at him—all gooey-eyed!"

He changed the subject then, talking about herself and her affairs with friendly interest—and when she mentioned that some of her letters from home had suggested she returned to Ireland, others that she went to Raballo, he told her, dismay in his tone, that he was hoping she had at last decided to settle down in Ste. Monique.

"If you leave here I've a feeling I'll never see you again," he said. "I couldn't bear that! Truly, Maura!"

His emotion was genuine and she couldn't help contrasting his attitude with Paul's. Never had Paul given the least sign of regret at the idea of parting from her for all time. Indeed he had shown an unflattering eagerness to rid the Caribbean of her unwelcome presence by providing her, openly or covertly, with the money for her return fare to Europe.

In her soreness of heart she felt drawn to him. She would never thrill to his voice, to his touch, but equally he would never have the power to make her suffer deeply.

There was something of the boy in his make-up, something that had little to do with age, and if she were to encourage him and eventually marry him, it would be she who would have to hold the boat steady, make the important decisions.

But would that matter if they were fond of each other—had the same idea of marriage as a permanent partnership, blessed with children?

Those words of Mrs. Gonzalez' rang in her brain: "Don't turn down a good man too readily... love may come!"

Absurd to think along those lines when Geoffrey had never told her he loved her, let alone wished to marry her. And yet with a woman's deep instinct she knew that if she wanted this genial, kindly, fair-haired young man for her husband, she could very quickly have him at her feet.

They danced together the whole evening to the sensuous throb of the steel band, sitting out, during the intervals, at tiny tables set under the palm trees. As always the air was heavy with the scent of flowering shrubs, and loud with the piping of bull-frogs.

"I sometimes think this island is sheer Paradise," she murmured after a while. "Or could be!"

"If one had love," was her unspoken thought, and at once Geoffrey responded wistfully: "If one had the right girl! The very beauty of it all emphasises one's loneliness."

Her mood changed at that.

"Come off it, Geoffrey," she said teasingly.

"You're never without a girl-friend—and never were, on that ship that brought us out here."

"They never come to anything, those friendships. I want something permanent. Don't you sometimes feel that way, Maura, in spite of all you've been through in the way of disillusionment?"

"I suppose so. But I'd rather remain unmarried than team up with the wrong man."

"But how is one to know? Maybe—" he took her hand in his, "you and I are right for each other. I'm a very ordinary chap, earning a very ordinary salary. But I'd realise what a treasure I'd found in you— work hard to get into a higher bracket—"

"You make me feel horribly mercenary," she exclaimed. "I'm a very simple person myself."

"You're a darling. And I've never seen a girl to touch you for looks." He was pulling her close to him, and the next moment had her in his arms, kissing her on her bare shoulder, her throat, her lips, murmuring passionately that he wanted her as he'd never wanted any woman before.

She struggled free, flushed and breathless, and he implored her not to be angry with him, declaring that he didn't mean to rush her.

"I'm not angry," she told him shakily. "But, Geoffrey, it's no good pretending, to you or to myself, that I love you—or ever will."

"Let's leave love out of it for the present," he urged. "Just go on being friends. But for goodness' sake put this idea of nursing in Raballo out of your head. We need the chance to know each other better."

She tried to tell him that there were reasons why she must leave Ste. Monique. That her peace of mind depended on it. But he would not let her—threatening, half laughing, to stop her mouth with kisses.

"Let's have no hard-and-fast decisions to-night," he insisted. And as the steel band started up again with its soft, compelling rhythm, he jumped up and drew her to her feet.

"You dance like a fairy," he said. "And maybe that's what you are. Too fine for poor, gross males who want to eat you up."

She did not reply, just smiled in what he thought, rather sorely, was an abstracted sort of way.

He would have felt far more sore if he had known what she was thinking—that his passionate kisses awoke no echo in her, only serving to show her with blinding clarity that she could never love him. That it was another man's kisses she ached for, and always would.

Even had she told him this, with brutal frankness, he would not, in his present mood, have taken her with complete seriousness. Time, he would have repeated, could work wonders.

She had arranged with Mr. Gonzalez to be back before midnight. Stella could not be left—there was still the fear of her waking up in a nightmare, screaming—and she did not want to force the child's father to stay up until the small hours.

To her relief Geoffrey did not exact a good-night kiss from her, and she was even more thankful for this when she saw Paul coming out of the hotel.

She would have passed him with a cool good-night, but he stopped her and asked her quietly if she could possibly spare him five minutes.

His expression told her that he had nothing very pleasant to say, and she was tempted to refuse. However, to do that would only be to postpone a conversation with him, and explaining coolly that she could give him just that time and no longer, since her employer would be up, waiting for her, she let him lead her to a secluded corner of the lounge.

There was dancing at the hotel, too, and the sounds of music drifted to them as they sat there—music which both found out of tune with their mood.

He lost no time in plunging into an appeal to her.

"Maura, you're making Phyllis terribly unhappy. Do you think it's sporting to take Geoffrey Fanshawe away from her?"

Her chin went up, and angry tears pricked her eyes.

"I've done nothing of the sort. If Phyllis had been better-tempered, and not so stupidly jealous, he'd still be going around with her."

"Maybe she is a little jealous—most people in love are inclined that way. But they'd have made up their differences if it hadn't been for you, and your readiness to step into her shoes."

Her blue eyes flashed now.

"You're grossly unfair to me. But then you always have been."

His expression changed.

"You're not going to tell me that you've fallen for the fellow yourself, Maura? If so—"

"I have not!" she snapped.

"Then let him go!"

"He's as free as air," she told him, still furiously angry with him. "And let me tell you, wealthy and successful as you are, you haven't the least understanding of human nature. If I rebuff Geoffrey and refuse the invitations which he presses on me, there's no guarantee that he'll go back to Phyllis. She's lousy to him whenever she sees him."

"Because she's feeling so sore. They were on the verge of getting engaged, you know."

"I didn't know. Anyway,"—and now it all came out in a burst—"she seems to be consoling herself very satisfactorily."

He gave her a sharp look.

"What do you mean by that?"

She shrugged her shoulders.

"Only that I happened to be looking out of my bedroom window the other night, and saw you kissing her. I suppose you'll tell me that you were just comforting her."

Her tone was scornful, but he did not show the embarrassment and confusion which she anticipated.

"You're perfectly right. So you've no need for all this shocked disapproval on poor Fanshawe's account."

His unwonted sarcasm stung her. She thought, with sudden horror, that he had pierced her secret, knew that her indignation was nothing more or less than the emotion of which she had accused Phyllis. Jealousy! Sheer, naked jealousy, which up to this moment she had fought against admitting to herself.

Desperate to hide it from him, she said icily: "All these tiresome appeals to me to send Geoffrey back to Phyllis leave me stone-cold. As it happens, I'm just completing my plans for leaving Ste. Monique and taking up work in Raballo."

"You can't mean it!" To her astonishment he had gone white with anger.

"I certainly do! Why, you suggested Raballo to me yourself, in your eagerness to push me out of Ste. Monique—"

"But you can't go there now!"

"What's stopping me?"

"What should stop you is a bit of decent feeling. Or don't you read the daily paper?"

Too furious to answer him, she jumped up, and walking quickly away to the lift was whirled up to her bedroom.

She found Mr. Gonzalez dozing in a wicker chair, and Stella peacefully asleep, and somehow managed to control her trembling.

Her employer had evidently been reading the newspapers, and when he roused up to ask her how she had enjoyed herself, and to take his departure to his own bedroom, she asked him to leave them with her —provided he had finished with them.

"Of course, my dear! But I guess you'd be wiser to get to sleep quickly than to start reading at this hour of the night."

She smiled non-committally, but the moment the door shut behind him she took them up and started looking through them systematically—one being yesterday's morning paper, the others to-day's issues.

Very soon she found what she was looking for—a paragraph, with an accompanying photograph, which gave the key to Paul's outrageous outburst.

The photograph was of Claude, debonair and smiling, and the letterpress told that a new branch of the Lasalle Plantations was being opened, rather unexpectedly, in Raballo, of which Claude Lasalle would be manager. He would be moving there from St. Jacques, with his wife and child, within the next few weeks.

She took out an air letter and wrote haltingly to Gwen that she could not come to Raballo.

CHAPTER 6

THERE was little sleep for Maura that night. Apart from her own anger and distress over Paul's cruel injustice, which kept her tossing and turning, Stella woke up before dawn in that ever-recurring nightmare, calling out to her mother's attacker—"Don't Manoel, *don't*!"

It was cool at this hour, and Maura took the little girl into her own bed under the white mosquito curtains, and soothed her to rest, singing under her breath the old Irish songs with which her own mother had lulled her in childhood days. And when at last sleep came and the dark lashes lay still on the small, rounded face, she carried her back to her own bed.

She tried now to sleep herself, murmuring the old Gaelic prayers which, too, had been part of her earliest memories. And for a while she succeeded. But with dawn came the usual clamour of cocks crowing in and around the city, and of dogs waking up one by one to bark their furious protests at this shrill shattering of the quiet.

As suddenly as they had begun the strident cock-a-doodle-do's died away, and with them the denunciatory yapping. All was silence.

But she could not drift into sleep again. Her mind was too active; she could not control its wanderings.

She tried not to think of Paul, nor of the fresh problem with which he had confronted her. This was no time to wrestle with distresses and dilemmas. But in whatever direction her thoughts went straying, she could find no peace.

When Stella stirred every now and then, she began to worry about Manoel's trial—to take place as soon as Mrs. Gonzalez was well enough to give evidence.

Dr. Craig had stressed the impossibility of involving Stella in any of the proceedings, though she had been the sole witness of the crime. And Mr. Gonzalez, ready to swear to his little daughter's cries, uttered as she was driven from the scene of the attack—cries of "Manoel, don't!"—had hinted to Maura that she might be required to corroborate his statement. Often enough she had heard those same incriminating words on Stella's lips—not in the hours of daylight, but when assailed, as an hour ago, by nightmare.

Shrinking from the ordeal of appearing in court, she recalled that cold, foggy morning in London when, knocked into the gutter by a ruffian who had snatched her bag, Paul had come to her help. She could remember every detail of that incident—the gentle strength with which Paul had picked her up and set her on her feet, the sympathy which he had shown her.

Clear as her memories were, they had an air of unreality. The Paul of those days, kindly, attractive, considerate, could he be the same person as the man who, ever since she had come to Ste. Monique, had treated her as a scheming adventuress?

Soon sunlight flooded the room, and from the Cathedral the silvery sound of the Angelus floated on the air, to be followed by the chiming of bells from all over the city.

They calmed her, for it was as though she were home in Ireland again—in Galway city, maybe, where she could not walk more than a few yards down the street without friendly greetings from folk who had known her since she was a child—where never, so long as she lived, could she have this terrible sense of being a stranger, and unwanted.

Before long, for the day starts early in the Caribbean, she had had her shower, and was helping Stella to dress. Mr. Gonzalez was always down to breakfast by half past seven, and liked to have his two "girls" with him.

But a few minutes before they were ready to go downstairs to the dining-room, while she was drying Stella after her bath, the telephone bell rang and Maura, answering it, heard Paul's voice on the line.

"Maura, I've rung up to apologise," he said hurriedly. "It was unpardonable of me to jump to the conclusion that your plan for going to Raballo had any connection with Claude's starting work there."

Because he had hurt her so badly—and maybe because of sheer exhaustion—she made what seemed the obvious reply.

"You've struck the right word—unpardonable."

"That's just what it was, I'm afraid. But it gave me such a shock. You see, I'd been largely responsible for sending Claude all those hundreds of miles away. It was quite clear to me, the last time I saw him, that he hadn't got you out of his system yet, and I thought it would be fairer all round—to you, Claude and Damaris—everybody."

"Claude is no danger to me," she said haughtily. "You must be very obtuse to think so, all this time."

"Sorry to keep saying the wrong thing, but I've hardly slept, worrying about our conversation last night. What I really mean is that Claude being so weak, and still not quite recovered from this infatuation for you, you're a danger to him and to his marriage. He and Damaris have been through the legal ceremony again and—"

"How many people am I supposed to be a danger to?" Maura exclaimed sharply. "Claude—Geoffrey—?"

"I might reply that you're a danger to any man," he said, trying to speak lightly. "But let's not quarrel. What I want to say is that Raballo is a very large island—at least six times as large as Ste. Monique and most of the other islands—and that if you've been offered a good post there it would be absurd for you to refuse it because of the very slight possibility of an encounter with Claude."

"In other words you're graciously giving me permission to go to Raballo," she retorted mockingly. "How very kind of you. But do you know this? I'm so sick and disgusted with the way I've been treated by you and your brother that I'm seriously considering going to the shipping office this very morning and fixing up my return to Ireland."

She was interrupted by a shrill cry.

"Maura! You can't go away. You can't, you can't!"

Stella had come in from the bathroom, half-dressed, and was staring at her in utter dismay.

At once Maura hung up the receiver and running over to the child dropped on her knees and put her arms round her.

"My darling, don't cry like that. You know that your Auntie Rita is coming very soon. You love her very, very much, don't you?"

The little girl nodded, the tears still flowing.

"But if you go to Ireland, I'll never see you again," she sobbed. "Papa says it's far, far away—much farther than Raballo. And that's far 'nuff."

"Well, don't let's worry about what may never happen." Maura hugged her very close. "My old granny used to say, 'One day at a time, child,' and it's a very good motto."

Stella looked puzzled.

"I thought mottoes came out of crackers at Christmas!"

"Maybe this one did—a very old Irish cracker! And now let's go down to breakfast, and make some lovely plans. What about asking some of the other children here to come on a picnic with us—taking cake and ice-cream and swim-suits?"

Stella's face had begun to lose its look of misery, and by the time they reached the dining-room most traces of tears had gone.

But her father's quick eyes observed that she had been crying, and after breakfast he managed to take Maura aside for a moment and asked her what had happened.

When Maura explained, he looked concerned.

"You've your own life to lead, of course," he said, "and it would be very wrong of me to try to stand in your way. But I do hope, for Stella's sake, that even when you leave her to the care of my sister, you'll be in touch with her until she settles down. She's very fond of her Aunt Rita, but lately you've meant so much to her."

Maura drew a deep breath.

"I'm undecided about my future," she told him. "There's a lot to consider. But I promise you this. I won't rush off at a moment's notice—to Raballo, or anywhere else."

"And my wife and I promise you this," he said, with Latin fervour. "Our gratitude and our friendship—always."

The picnic party which Maura had promised Stella turned out a far larger affair than she had planned. All the children who were staying at the hotel wanted to take part, some of them demanding that their young mothers came, too; and at the last minute the manager of the hotel, discovering that twin boys were celebrating their sixth birthday, added a big box of toys to the well-stocked baskets of refreshments, and told Phyllis Reeves he wished her to share in the entertainment of the small guests.

Maura decided to make the best of this unwelcome development. She could not herself withdraw, and she knew that Phyllis was bound to carry out the manager's instructions and, furthermore, to promote a friendly, happy atmosphere.

By good luck she saw her alone for a minute, closing up her desk, and asked if she could speak to her.

"I've only a second to spare, if that's any good to you," was Phyllis's cool response. "The cook has just sent for me. Something about the refreshments for this party you've wished on us."

"All I have to say is that I'll do my best to cooperate with you in any way I can," Maura said quickly. "We don't want outsiders—children or grown-ups—to see that we aren't on the best of terms."

Phyllis looked at her for a moment in silence. Then she said: "Paul says I've misjudged you. I wish I could feel that way. I used to like you so much."

"I've never stopped liking you," Maura told her. "It hurts me that you distrust me."

Phyllis shrugged her shoulders.

"I just can't help it. But I'll try to forget it for to-day—pretend we're back on the liner that brought us out from home."

She played up well, and no one going off for that picnic could have imagined that there was any cloud in the friendship between the two girls. In the gayest of spirits, apparently, they swept the dozen or so children, and the two mothers who had volunteered to accompany them, into the three big cars at their disposal, and with much singing and laughter set out in file for the beach which Phyllis had decided was most suitable.

It was one of those glorious afternoons so common in the Caribbean as to evoke no remark except from passing strangers. Above, the deep blue sky, flecked with the occasional small white cloud, and on either side of the road, tall trees with coral-coloured blossoms—*immortelles*, planted there not merely to flaunt their beauty against that azure backcloth but to shade the tender cocoa plants from the direct rays of the sun.

Cool trade winds tempered the heat, and as the road switchbacked through forests, cleared here and there for crops, the stretches of green were gemmed with other flowering trees, their blossoms of pink or gold, blue or crimson, gleaming like jewels against emerald-hued velvet.

If there was an earthly Paradise, surely it was here, Maura thought, sitting with Stella and the twin boys in the car which Phyllis was driving. And yet, high up on the mountain side, miles off still, but clearly visible, was the low white building where Manoel was awaiting trial, where condemned criminals lived out their days behind blind walls, as cut off from beauty and from their fellow-men as in any city gaol.

After climbing for a while the road swept down to the long sandy beach, fringed with palm trees, which was their destination, and in no time everyone was out of the car, the elders unpacking the hampers, the children rushing down to the shore, the little ones to paddle, the bigger boys to throw rocks up at the coconuts.

"Tea" came first—with iced drinks, jellies and pastries, and a splendid iced birthday cake concocted at short notice by the hotel chef. Then rounders, and finally the longed-for bathe.

At Phyllis's suggestion, each grown-up superintended one small group of children, for while there was no fear of sharks—warm as the water was—the sand shelved steeply here and there, and in one direction there was a pole to mark where a current ran.

The water was so pleasant, so buoyant that they could have stayed there for hours, plunging into the sea and then, emerging, lying to dry on the hot sand. But Phyllis and Maura, well aware how quickly darkness could fall, began soon after five o'clock to gather the children together in readiness for the homeward journey.

And then suddenly Phyllis, turning towards the sea, gave a cry of horror. One of the twin boys had run back into the sea, in the forbidden direction, had lost his foothold, and was being swept towards the warning flag-pole.

She was into the water at once, followed closely by the child's agonised mother, and swimming strongly reached the little boy about the same moment. His mother grabbed him, and with Phyllis's help got him on her shoulders and started back for the beach. But the effort Phyllis had made precipitated another crisis. One of her arms went up in a desperate gesture as she disappeared from view, and now Maura, freeing herself from Stella who was clinging to her, and exclaiming: "It's O.K., darling, don't be scared," went plunging into the sea.

But for Phyllis's steadiness of nerve both girls would certainly have drowned; but surfacing for a second time, she managed to obey Maura's sharp directions, threw herself on her back, so that she was floating instead of struggling, and with Maura also on her back, swimming hard, was brought to safety.

But her ashen look as she collapsed on the beach made Maura wonder in terror if the rescue had been too late. She had passed right out and her look was that of a person who had been drowned.

Thankful for those lessons in life-saving which she had learnt in London, Maura lost not a moment in starting "the kiss of life," breathing rhythmically and with studied pauses into Phyllis's colourless lips, until at last signs of life returned.

Soon she was bringing up the salt water she had swallowed, and wrapped in dry towels was being carried to one of the cars, with Maura at the wheel, Stella close to her again.

The cavalcade reached the hotel in a far from jaunty mood. Relief was the key-note, and some of the smaller children, including Stella, had dropped off to sleep.

Fortunately Mr. Gonzalez was at the entrance, looking out for them. He had had no idea of anything being wrong, but quickly took charge of Stella, leaving Maura free to devote herself to Phyllis.

In a short time she had her patient lying comfortably on her small white bed, and had persuaded her to sip some hot, sweet tea. And presently she was rewarded by a grateful glance from the girl's shadowed eyes.

"If it wasn't for you, I'd be dead," Phyllis murmured. "I got cramp in one of my legs. It was terrifying—feeling that I was being swept nearer and nearer that awful current." And then she added, the slow, difficult tears forcing themselves from under her purple lids: "It was my fault, really, choosing that beach. But the other end of the bay, where we were all bathing, is perfectly safe. I ought to have realised that with small children there might be a risk."

"You've nothing to reproach yourself with, Phyl," Maura assured her earnestly. "Personally I think you're a heroine. To go down twice, and then have the courage and presence of mind to do exactly what you were told—!" And she added, after a moment: "Most people would have clung to the person who was trying to help them. If you'd done that—well, neither of us would be here."

Within the hour the Press was on the track of the party. Fortunately the mother of the twins had no objection to giving interviews, and after fruitless efforts to contact Phyllis and Maura the reporters left to get the story into the late extra editions, and they were left in peace.

As soon as she had settled Phyllis down for the night Maura went up, with some trepidation, to find Stella. Although she had remained very quiet during all the excitements on the beach, Maura knew that she had been very frightened indeed, and was horribly afraid of a setback to her slow recovery from that terrible night of the attack on her mother.

She found her in bed and asleep under the mosquito curtain, with her father sitting beside her.

"She's all right," he whispered. "A bit shaken, of course. But she has such faith in you, Maura, that she knew for certain—so she told me—that you'd be all right." And then he added, scowling: "I gather from what she said that the whole thing started with one of those twin boys running back into the sea. I shall have something to say to his mother—endangering so many lives by her carelessness in not looking after her children properly."

Maura shook her dark head.

"I shouldn't! She's had a lesson she'll never forget. We're all safe and sound, and personally I'd rather think no more about it."

That night Stella awoke again in a nightmare, but it was evident that the day's happenings had not given her fresh horrors to combat. The cry was the same as ever: "Don't, Manoel, *don't*!" And before Maura could go to her it had died away and the child was asleep again.

Next morning the *Belleray Herald* splashed the story on the front page, the information having been given, she saw, by the mother of the twins. It was a somewhat highly-coloured account of the incidents, but fairly accurate, and though she felt uncomfortable at the praise which was showered on her for her courage and presence of mind, she could find little to criticise.

But she was sharply annoyed at the photographs of herself and Phyllis standing together in their swim-suits. The caption conveyed that the pictures had been taken the previous afternoon, but she recognised instantly, being actually in possession of the prints, that it was Geoffrey who had taken them, months ago, by the swimming pool of the liner which had brought them all from England.

He had had no right, she considered, to hand these prints over to the Press without permission, nor to give the irrelevant details about herself and her career which appeared at the end of the column.

It gave her no pleasure whatever to read that she was a beautiful raven-haired, blue-eyed colleen, the darling of a large farming family in Galway, who had left her native land to train in one of London's most famous hospitals. That the people of Ste. Monique should be proud to have such a brilliant and experienced young nurse settling down to work in their island home.

She was slightly vexed, when she went to settle Phyllis in a wicker chair on a back veranda, that the other girl thought her irritation with Geoffrey unreasonable.

"If Geoff hadn't helped the reporters they would have worried us to death for a story," she pointed out. And when, just as she was speaking, he turned up beaming, with sheaves of flowers for his two "heroines," and the explanation that he had indeed fended off the Press the previous evening, she behaved more graciously to him than for some time past.

He knew one of the senior reporters, he told them —that was how he had managed to have them left in peace. But Maura was not to be placated. She did not go to the length of refusing his flowers, but she told him shortly that she would have preferred him to discuss the matter with her, and went off leaving him and Phyllis to shake their heads over her surprising display of ill-temper.

She had to admit to herself that she might be behaving a little unreasonably in her strong dislike of being thrust into the public eye. Certainly Mr. Gonzalez thought so when she discussed the matter with him. And though she had no direct reaction from Paul, his mother, laid up with some small ailment in the Lasalle country home, took the trouble to ring up and congratulate her warmly on her courage and presence of mind.

"I suppose I'm a fool," she decided at length. "What harm can a little silly publicity do me?"

And little guessed what the answer to this purely rhetorical question would be.

CHAPTER 7

LOVING Stella as she did, it was yet a relief to Maura when the child's aunt arrived from South America a little earlier than expected, to take charge of her, and to open up the Gonzalez home at the other side of the island.

She was a friendly, capable young woman, of twenty-seven or so, this "Aunt Rita," very fond of her niece, and most anxious to show appreciation of Maura's care and devotion.

"I don't want you to go rushing off now that I've come," she told her the following morning. "The break would be too sudden for Stella. Indeed I'm wondering if you could bring her with you when I drive over to Villa Bianca to arrange alterations there."

Maura looked doubtful, afraid of the effect the very sight of the house might have on the small girl. But Rita Gonzalez pointed out sensibly that Stella would have to go there some time or other, unless her brother decided to sell the house and move, and that to get used to it before actually staying there might help her to settle down.

"Both she and her parents will be sleeping in a different wing," she explained. "Even so my brother wants me to have the rooms redecorated, and furnished with new, modern stuff, so that there will be nothing to remind her of her terrible experience. The wing where the awful thing happened will also be made unrecognisable—turned into reception rooms, I believe."

"Wouldn't it be better for Stella to put off going to the Villa until the changes have actually been made?" Maura queried.

Rita shrugged her shapely shoulders.

"What's to happen to the child meantime? The conversion will take a month at the very least. And we can't expect you, a valuable trained nurse, to stay around, wasting your time and talents."

"Suppose she—and her mother, too—find it impossible to settle down there?" Maura asked the question nervously, afraid of appearing officious.

"My dear, in that case the family would probably dig up its roots, and come back to the Argentine," Rita told her, adding gaily, "And if they did that, you might consider coming out to South America, too. I'm sure there's more scope for an English-trained S.R.N. out there than in this small island. However, you may have other plans. I expect you feel as I do—" and she flung out her arms in a typically Latin gesture, " 'the world's my oyster' !"

A few days later, after some fevered shopping in Belleray's best store, the two girls took Stella with them to the Villa Bianca. The low Colonial house, set within brilliantly flowering hibiscus hedges, looked very peaceful in the sunshine, and though Stella, walking between them, clutched their hands as they went through the open front door, she relaxed as the fat, smiling cook, her head tied up in a red bandana handkerchief, came waddling out to greet her and fold her to her capacious bosom.

The butler, Cook's husband, hurried along, too, to announce that everything was ready for their picnic in the back veranda—apologising for his rough clothes, with the explanation that there was "plentee, plentee cleanin'" to be done before the fine new furniture arrived.

In the interest and excitement of changing the house around, all signs of tenseness on Stella's part vanished completely, and on the long drive back to Belleray, as the child alternately chattered and slept, Maura realised that her job with the Gonzalez family was nearing its end. She had finished her task, and all should now be well with them.

A letter with a local stamp was waiting for her at the hotel when the three of them returned there—a letter which gave further impetus to her intention to move on to fresh fields.

Mrs. Martin wanted her to return at the first possible moment to take on a private patient. She had no other nurse to spare, and would be in a bad fix if Maura delayed coming.

The appeal decided her. She had stayed away from Hillside longer than at first arranged, and things being as they were, it was high time she went back.

A contributory cause to her wish to leave the Florida-Carib as soon as decently possible was the feeling that once she was out of the way the friendship between Geoffrey and Phyllis, which had begun to mend after that drama on the beach, would have a good chance of healing completely.

Phyllis was utterly different now, in her attitude to Maura: all traces of distrust and hostility had gone. But Geoffrey had not quite recovered from the scolding she had given him over handing photographs to the Press, and was slightly embarrassed in her company. The sooner she left them to themselves the better. Geoffrey could then renew his attentions to his first love without feeling foolish.

She tried to stifle a sharp regret that she would be unlikely to see anything of Paul, once she left the Florida-Carib. Although he lived out in the country with his mother, he used the hotel almost as a club, and was often in and out.

Catching these odd glimpses of him should not make any difference to her, for they seldom exchanged a word. He had been away at the time of the ill-fated picnic, and though he had stopped her on his return, days later, to congratulate her stiffly for her "wonderful life-saving exploits" she felt that he had spoken only from forced politeness.

Mr. Gonzalez himself drove her back to Hillside, where Mrs. Martin had managed to arrange a bedroom for her, and was able to assure her that she would not have to appear in court when Manoel was brought up for trial.

"I only wish my poor wife could have been spared the ordeal," he sighed. "But the doctors say she will be reasonably fit in a fortnight's time. At least my poor little Stella won't be called."

And once again he assured her of his gratitude for all she had done to help and steady the child.

Mrs. Martin's welcome to her bordered on the effusive, but Raymonde's could hardly have been more casual, and Maura very soon learnt the reason for her unfriendliness.

The patient whom she was to take on was, of all people, Paul's stepmother, Mrs. Lasalle, who was laid up with an attack of cardiac asthma.

For two days, it seemed, Raymonde had been looking after her, but this arrangement had proved most unsatisfactory. Mrs. Lasalle had made no complaint, but Dr. Craig, in attendance on her, had declared that unless his orders were carried out to the letter he would arrange that Mrs. Lasalle was transferred to the private wing of the General Hospital.

"Raymonde was furious at his tone." Mrs. Martin motioned Maura to sit down at the other side of the desk. "She actually wanted me to tell Dr. Craig— 'Go ahead! Take Mrs. Lasalle away!' But she pulled herself together when I reminded her pretty sharply what Hillside owed to Paul. After all, she herself has some capital invested in the home—unfortunately!"

"What was the actual trouble?" Maura asked, a shade diffidently.

"Inexcusable carelessness. She was late giving Mrs. Lasalle her adrenalin injection. Even now she refuses to admit that a mistake like that matters."

"Why not suggest her going to England or America for a first-rate training? That would pull her up!"

"She'd never accept the discipline," was Mrs. Martin's bitter reply. "Besides, she finds the life out here far too enjoyable. She's my own niece, but I heartily regret having let her put money into the home. If it wasn't for the scandal it would cause, I'd try to buy her out."

For a moment Maura was silent. Then she said: "It's going to be a little awkward for me, taking over her patient. And to tell you the truth I'm not on very good terms with Paul Lasalle."

"Personal feelings have nothing to do with your work," Mrs. Martin returned loftily. "If Raymonde gives you any trouble, you must let me know at once, so that I can deal with her. As for Paul, I happen to know that whatever he thinks of you as a woman, he has great respect for you as a nurse."

Since there was plainly no more to be said Maura went to change into uniform and on the way met Sister Baker, the elderly S.R.N. whom Dr. Craig had found for Mrs. Martin some weeks earlier.

"My dear, am I glad to see you?" Sister Baker exclaimed. "That Raymonde! She's the most incompetent, unfeeling creature I ever nursed with. And her tongue! You look out for her. The things she says about you!"

Maura managed to smile.

"I don't think I shall lose much sleep over Raymonde," she said, as casually as she could, but didn't feel too happy as she went on her way.

She ought not to worry. She had nothing to be ashamed of. But the odd hint, the odd lie, could put her actions in a very ugly light.

Suppose the false story got around that she had known, before she came out to the Caribbean, that Claude Lasalle, the man she was engaged to, had recently been divorced by a young impetuous wife who now wanted him back? That she, an Irish girl, had schemed to keep him away from his former wife and small son!

Suppose, even, that Raymonde had circulated the cruel rumour that she had come between Geoffrey Fanshawe and Phyllis Reeves!

It wouldn't be quite so horrible if these things were said in the open—but to have them whispered behind her back, without giving her a chance to rebut them!

But the welcome which Mrs. Lasalle gave her, as soon as she went into her room, chased away the hobgoblins.

"My dear, I'm delighted to see you," the sick

woman told her, smiling and holding out her hand. "And Paul—he'll be so relieved. He knew you'd be back very soon, or he wouldn't have let me come here. But I expect Mrs. Martin explained all that."

"More or less." Maura could hardly comment that Mrs. Martin was seldom completely candid. "And now if you're comfortable I'll ring Dr. Craig. I'd like to have his instructions direct."

It was a great change from looking after little Stella, but though she missed the child's clinging arms, and soft kisses, she was glad to be doing a professional job once more.

And she could hardly have had a more satisfactory patient than Mrs. Lasalle—or a more appreciative one.

Since Dr. Craig, who called daily, had enjoined quiet, Mrs. Lasalle had few visitors and then for very short periods only. But, as she told Maura, she did not mind. The only person she would have been eager to see was her beloved Paul; and he was far away in Raballo, helping Claude with the beginnings of the new branch there.

"Claude's my own, and I love him dearly," she said one day when Maura was moving around setting the room to rights. "But I've had so much trouble with him." She hesitated, then added quietly: "I can never forget the abominable way he treated you. He admitted it to me himself, once he knew Paul had spoken to me about it. And I told him in no uncertain terms exactly what I thought about it."

"That's over and done with." Maura flicked her duster round with even greater energy. "I went through a bad time, until I realised that I had never really loved him—that I'd simply fallen for his charm."

"You're a grand girl, Maura. If you'd known him when he was younger you might have managed him better than poor Damaris has done. But it's a mercy that you came through so well and without bitterness: that you're happy now."

"If you only knew!" Maura thought, resisting the insidious temptation to lead the conversation back to Paul. But when Mrs. Lasalle, after dozing off for a while, began to speak of her stepson it was in terms which Maura found hard to accept.

In Mrs. Lasalle's eyes he was by no means faultless. He was too impetuous, too ready to jump to conclusions—false conclusions, sometimes. But he was fundamentally sound, she declared, straight as a die, and his hidden acts of generosity were past counting. People called him cold and reserved, and certainly he had never had the social success of his half-brother. Still, the people who worked under him thought the world of him. He was the first person to whom they turned in trouble.

Remembering Paul's wounding suspicions of her, Maura found it impossible to make an enthusiastic response, and while she was searching for something to say—polite nothings—Mrs. Lasalle gave her a keen look.

"You don't like him," she said reflectively. "I wonder why!"

"One can't analyse these things," was Maura's carefully controlled reply. "Anyway, he's given me plenty of proof that it's mutual."

Mrs. Lasalle looked puzzled.

"He's never talked to me about you, except as a nurse. Being highly efficient himself he admires that quality very much in other people."

"That has nothing to do with liking or disliking,"

Maura pointed out with an effort at lightness. "But, Mrs. Lasalle, you'll be getting tired with all this talking. I want you to settle down and get a real sleep. Rest is an all-important part of your cure."

Mrs. Lasalle, letting her arrange the pillows, smiled up at her.

"Whatever Paul thinks about you, I know this," she said. "I liked you from the first moment I met you—and I always shall."

"And I you!" Maura returned, smothering the impulse to bend down and kiss the pale cheek.

That, she told herself, was a gesture that might be misunderstood—giving the idea that she would welcome a more personal relationship with her patient.

And she crimsoned as she thought how shaming it would be if Paul were to stumble on her secret—realise that while she could with truth maintain that she did not "like" him, a far stronger emotion was threatening to sweep her off her feet, making all his faults, his injustice, his cruel suspicions, of no account.

Leaving the invalid with a bell-pull within easy reach, she went to settle herself into the little room which Mrs. Martin had assigned to her, and then went out into the garden for a spell of fresh air.

She sat there for a while, at the back of the house, glancing through the daily paper and taking no particular interest in the occasional car which drove up to the front entrance. And then a shadow fell across the paper and glancing up she saw Paul standing there.

"I've just been to see my stepmother," he said, and it seemed to her that he was just as nervous and embarrassed as she was. "She told me I'd find you out here, resting."

"If she's awake, I'd better go in to her!" Maura,

getting up out of the very low wicker chair, hardly needed help. But he took her hands and pulled her up, asking her with a faint smile: "Does this remind you of anything?"

"Oh, yes! Of your lifting me out of the gutter. But I'd have got to my feet then, as now, without your help."

"Must you bite my head off every time we meet?" he demanded. "I came out here to tell you how thankful I am you are looking after Mother. And I wanted, also, a chance to congratulate you—properly —on that wonderful rescue feat—snatching Phyllis out of that frightful current, and then giving her the kiss of life. I'm proud to know you, Maura."

"I've always been a strong swimmer." Sheer nervousness at his closeness made her speak stiffly. "As for the kiss of life, we learn that as a matter of course when we're training."

"You're very unfriendly, Maura. I'm here literally on a flying visit—to see Mother. Shan't be back for a month. Won't you forgive me before I go?"

But for the slightly teasing note in his voice she would have relaxed, obeyed that strong impulse to go straight into his arms. He had touched her quick Irish pride, however, and she flared up.

"You're not really sorry," she exclaimed under her breath. "You lifted me out of a London gutter once— and you're still doing the King Cophetua act. Thinking you can make up for your horrible unkindness by offering to pay my fare home, and when I refuse, going behind my back and bribing Mrs. Martin to raise my salary."

He went white.

"You're a bitter, unreasonable little vixen," he said sharply.

She shrugged her shoulders.

"Whom you'll soon forget! I'll not be in the Caribbean much longer."

"Well, I'll have one memory! I don't know much about the kiss of life. But there's another kind. This!"

And before she could resist him he had pulled her into his arms and kissed her hard, full on the lips. Then freeing her, he went striding off, and the next moment she heard him start up his car and drive away.

She stood there for a full minute, shaken with an emotion which scared her by its violence. She ought to be angry, furious at his kissing her in full view of the windows of the Nursing Home, humiliated by his cavalier treatment.

"So I am!" she told herself desperately. "These kiss-and-ride-away types, who think any girl is glad of their attentions!"

But deep in her heart there were very different feelings—feelings which Geoffrey's ardour had certainly not awakened, nor Claude's caresses. Passion, yes! But with it a strange, unreasoning tenderness which was surely neither deserved—nor wanted!

A few minutes later when she went along to her patient she was, to all appearances, her usual calm, efficient self—able, even, to agree prettily with Mrs. Lasalle that it had been a pleasant surprise all round, Paul's sudden call at Hillside.

She suspected that the older woman would have liked to know just how her brief encounter with Paul had gone. But she was too courteous to pry, and with good reason Maura, for her part, preferred to maintain an oyster-like silence.

She found it easy to devote herself to her patient: she had never nursed anyone so sweet-tempered and considerate, so smiling in pain and discomfort. And when at the end of a month, Paul still being away in Raballo, Dr. Craig pronounced her fit to go home, Maura, after a moment of hesitation, agreed to go with her for a night or two, and settle her in.

It would be a relief, she felt, to get away from the nursing home, from Raymonde's all too obvious jealousy, and Mrs. Martin's rather fulsome compliments. And up there, in the peace and quiet of the Lasalle home, she could perhaps come to a definite decision on the future—whether to go back to Galway, where the warmest welcome awaited her from her family, or to follow up the suggestion of the Gonzalez family that she should take up a nursing job in South America.

She noticed, when the Lasalle car came to fetch her and her patient, that a different chauffeur was driving, and commented on this to Mrs. Lasalle.

"I'll explain later," Mrs. Lasalle murmured, but the new chauffeur, in uninhibited West Indian fashion, remarked over his shoulder: "Mister Paul done give dat fellow de push las' time he over from Raballo. Too much drinkin'. Mah sister cook up dere, an' she speak fo' me."

"My stepson told me about it on that last flying visit of his," Mrs. Lasalle returned quietly, adding kindly: "You certainly drive well, Ben."

The man nodded cheerfully.

"I very good, very careful driver, ma'am! Stay wit' you long time, please de Lawd!"

It was very pleasant, Maura found, to be staying in the gracious Lasalle house, with its wide wooden balconies and beautiful old French furniture, its garden, full of tropical flowers and trees bright with blossom, and quiet but for the fluting calls of gay-coloured birds.

The staff, too, was welcoming and most competent, and it was clear that strong affection existed between them and their employers, all of them showing the greatest delight at having Mrs. Lasalle back, in much-improved health.

In order to be near her Maura had been installed in Paul's study-cum-dressing-room, both this room and Mrs. Lasalle's bedroom, leading out on to the same balcony, at the side of the house, with a fine view over the forest-covered mountains.

"The staff sleep right out at the back," Mrs. Lasalle explained, as they drank their after-dinner coffee in the spacious drawing-room, hung with family portraits. "And though I'm not nervous as a rule, it's nice, for a night or two, to have you within call. After that, Paul will be home—so he says in his last letter—and while I'd be delighted for you to stay on I'd put you in a more feminine room."

Nothing would have induced Maura to admit, even to herself, that it gave her a thrill to be sleeping in this room which demonstrated so clearly Paul's ownership.

There were his tennis-racquets in one corner, in another, under-water equipment and a sporting gun. One wall was lined with books dealing, she observed, with a wide variety of subjects, and the stretcher bed, under the white mosquito net, could hardly have been more austere.

The butler, rather a grand name for the toothless old gentleman who had served the Lasalle family in one capacity or another for the last forty years, was in charge of all the locking-up, and he did it last thing, most thoroughly. But as she watched him securing the door and windows of her room, and Mrs. Lasalle's, Maura could not help thinking that a determined marauder, especially one who knew the house, would hardly be deterred by all these precautions. These picturesque old wooden buildings with their wide verandas dripping with creepers were matchbox affairs in comparison with the modern structures of concrete and metal going up now all over the island.

Truth to tell she had begun to think, with a trepidation she concealed from Mrs. Lasalle, of that horrible affair in the Gonzalez home when a disgruntled gardener who had been dismissed had broken in on a thieving expedition, and had nearly killed his former employer's wife.

Wasn't the stage set here for a similar crime? The master of the house away, Mrs. Lasalle sleeping alone in this part of the house, except for a young nurse, none of the staff being within call—and a chauffeur, recently sacked, who doubtless harboured a strong grievance.

"I'm being absurd," she told herself, as she undressed and climbed into bed. "The very fact of Manoel's arrest and probable imprisonment for years would make anyone with similar plans think twice. It can't be such an out-of-the-way thing for an employee to be sent away if he doesn't behave himself."

She tried desperately to shake off her fears, and get to sleep. But the old wooden walls and furniture creaked with the cooling of the temperature, and she tossed and turned, haunted by that ever-recurring shriek of Stella's *"Manoel, don't!"*

At last she dropped off, but later was rudely awakened by stealthy but distinct movements on the balcony outside. This, too, had shuttered windows, and a door leading to an outer staircase, but in spite of old Ben's locking someone had got in and was now creeping along—yes, and trying, very quietly, the handle of her door. Too terrified to move, she saw by a ray of moonlight which stole through a half-open shutter that a knife blade was being inserted to prise the door open, and at that she jumped out of bed and running for the gun which stood in the corner, thrust the muzzle through the open shutter.

"I've a gun," she called out. "If you don't clear off this minute I'm shooting."

"Look out, it's loaded!" came a familiar voice. But even while Paul was speaking, Maura, drawing back cautiously from the window, tripped over a footstool, and the gun went off.

As the shot rang out, she heard a cry, followed by a low groan. And rushing to unlock the door she saw Paul leaning against the wooden wall in the half-light, his face distorted with pain.

CHAPTER 8

SHE switched on the lights and ran to him.

"Paul! Where did the shot go?"

"Into my shoulder!" He was straightening himself, forcing a grin on to his face. "What a girl!"

"I thought you were that chauffeur you sacked, breaking in—like the gardener at the Gonzalez house." The shock was so intense she could scarcely keep her teeth from chattering. And then, her nursing training reasserting itself, she went on quickly: "Come inside. I must try to stop the bleeding."

Amazingly, no one in the house seemed to have heard the shot. No sound issued from Mrs. Lasalle's room nor from the staff quarters at the back: no lights came on.

She got him into the bathroom, ripped off his shirt, and managed with a towel to stop the flow of blood. Then she helped him on to his bed—the bed which she herself had just left—and propped him up with pillows.

"I'll telephone the hospital to fetch you in an ambulance," she said. "They'll have to get the shot out."

"All that can wait until morning." His tone was imperious. "I won't have the household roused up just because I've been peppered by a shotgun."

"I might have killed you!"

"Oh, rubbish! It's nothing, Maura. Don't fuss!"

His very irascibility helped to steady her. She said coolly: "I'm not fussing. But I'm going down to the kitchen to get us both a hot drink."

He made no response to this, and she stole downstairs, with only a vague idea where the kitchen was placed, but switching on lights as she went.

Finding it, she soon collected the wherewithal for making tea, and in a few minutes was creeping upstairs again with a tray.

The hot, sweet drink brought a little colour to his cheeks. He asked, blinking in a dazed sort of way: "Incidentally, Maura, what on earth are you doing here, sleeping in my dressing-room?"

"Dr. Craig said your stepmother was well enough to leave the nursing home, and she was keen to come. But she was nervous of sleeping alone."

He frowned.

"I cabled that I'd be back in the small hours. We've an arrangement that when I can't reach home until very late she leaves that door on the veranda unlocked." He added grumpily: "I suppose the message is sitting in the cable office."

"You shouldn't keep talking," Maura told him in professional tones. "Swallow those tablets. They'll ease the pain."

"What are they?" He achieved that sardonic grin again. "You've shot me. How do I know that you're not finishing me off with a dose of poison? After all, you've never disguised your dislike of me."

"I could say the same about you. But that's enough of personalities. Please try to relax. I'm going to finish what's left of the night in the drawing-room."

Dawn was already silvering the sky as she stole downstairs, and curled up on a settee she heard the shrill sound of cockcrow from distant villages, followed by the inevitable protest of the local dogs. Then silence for a while until, the sky flushed to rose, morning came as always with fresh clamour from the cocks, and a high-toned bell ringing out the Angelus.

She went up quietly then to take a look at Paul, who was awake, and clearly in pain.

"I'm going now to tell your stepmother what has happened, and to call the ambulance," she said. "It's high time you were having proper attention."

"You've done pretty well yourself so far, Maura," was his reply—in a much weaker voice, she noticed. "What about my staying here, and you nursing me? I'd be a very docile patient—or—" and he smiled feebly—"would I?"

She shook her head.

"It's the hospital for you, I'm afraid. And—and, Paul, I'm terribly sorry for being such a fool."

"What do you mean by that?" As he leaned forward eagerly, pain caught him; he gave an uncontrollable little cry.

"For tripping and letting off the gun, of course," she returned quickly. "But please keep quiet."

"I see. I thought perhaps you meant something else," he murmured. "Okay, tell Mother. But don't agitate her. You know—her heart and all that!"

"I've been nursing her for weeks," she reminded him with a trace of hauteur, and went off to see Mrs. Lasalle.

Lena, the housemaid—another of Cook's numerous relations—had just gone in to Mrs. Lasalle's room with a tray of tea, and was babbling away excitedly about someone having already been in the kitchen making tea.

"I went down in the small hours," Maura explained, and as Lena disappeared she told Mrs. Lasalle, with the feeling of being the world's fool, just what had happened while she and the rest of the household were peacefully asleep.

Mrs. Lasalle stared at her in bewilderment and set down her tea-cup with a clatter.

"I don't blame you, child. It must have been terrible for you, the gun going off like that and wounding him. But surely you should have sent for the ambulance right away!"

"He absolutely forbade me to do anything before daylight," Maura explained. "Of course if I'd hit him in a vital spot I'd have ignored his orders. As it was I dared not excite him by opposing him outright." She took up the telephone receiver. "I'll ring from here, if I may."

Within a few minutes everyone in the house had heard of the accident and was discussing it in low excited tones. Breakfast trays appeared as though by magic. And in less than an hour Paul was being carried down from his dressing-room in a stretcher and placed carefully in the ambulance.

At his request both Mrs. Lasalle and Maura accompanied him to the big hospital in Belleray. But when they learned that there was nothing they could do, they went back by car—the chauffeur having insisted on following them down—only stopping on the way long enough to order flowers and fruit to be sent in for Paul, and to cable Claude a reassuring account of the accident.

"The papers will get hold of the story in no time," Mrs. Lasalle explained, "and goodness knows what they'll put in. I don't want him rushing over from Raballo expecting to find Paul in a dying condition. Indeed, I don't want him rushing back at all."

Although they had been away from the house for so short a time, they arrived back to find that the missing cable had just been delivered, and that reporters and camera-men were turning up hot on the scent of a good news story.

At the time of the swimming incident, when Maura had rescued Phyllis Reeves from drowning, bringing her round with the kiss of life, she had escaped the worst of the publicity by simply sheltering in the hotel. Here she could not avoid the full limelight, and on Mrs. Lasalle's advice she gave the reporters a short, accurate story, and allowed herself to be photographed, stipulating that Mrs. Lasalle should also be in the picture.

When things had simmered down a little Maura was able to give her former patient her full attention, persuading her to rest and to let old Ben, the butler, to answer, with a stereotyped reply, the many telephone enquiries which now began.

Running true to form, Mrs. Lasalle's concern was all for Paul, suffering in hospital, and for Maura who, in a different way, was enduring just as much distress. Herself she did not consider at all, but realising how much it would mean to Maura, she allowed her to fuss over her a little, as though she were still employed as her regular nurse.

"I want you to stay with me, Maura," she said, as the two of them sat toying with their lunch on the back veranda. "As you can imagine, I don't feel like being left. Mrs. Martin won't mind, I'm sure. In any case I'll make it all right with her."

Maura's eyes brimmed with tears.

"You're so sweet to me," she stammered. "You might easily have been furious with me for behaving so idiotically. But it was those weeks with Stella, when she was having constant nightmares about Manoel's attack on her mother—! They affected me, I suppose, in a way I didn't expect. I was terrified when I realised someone was trying to prise open the lock of my door in what seemed the middle of the night." She hesitated. "It wasn't just for myself, I was scared. I thought that chauffeur you'd dismissed might have a grudge against you—might half-kill you."

"My dear, I understand everything. I don't blame you at all. If anyone is at fault it's Paul himself for leaving his gun loaded. And so I shall tell him when he's better. But let's keep to the point. You'll stay on with me until he comes back, won't you?"

Maura was glad to agree. Up here, with Mrs. Lasalle, she would hear at once every detail of Paul's progress, would probably be able to go with her to visit Paul. And apart from that, it was very restful being in Mrs. Lasalle's company, in this cool, spacious house set in its flower-filled garden, waited on by Cook and her smiling relatives.

All fear of intruders had vanished. For as old Ben pointed out wisely, bad men would be careful to keep away knowing that there was a lady in the house who was "plenty quick wit' de trigger!"

But she was not destined to settle down for more than a day or two. At the end of that time a cable came from Claude, announcing that he and Damaris, with their little boy, were on the point of flying over to stay with Mrs. Lasalle, and learn at first hand just how Paul was faring.

She most definitely, she told Mrs. Lasalle, didn't wish to meet Claude and his family. And Mrs. Lasalle, though annoyed with Claude for rushing over, and certain that Paul would be annoyed, too, could only agree to her leaving at once.

Back she went to Hillside, to find to her dismay that Mrs. Martin had been summoned to St. Jacques through the illness of a relative, leaving Sister Baker in charge of the nursing arrangements and Raymonde to run the domestic side.

Sister Baker and the other nurses at Hillside gave her a delighted welcome, but Raymonde, greeting her coldly, told her that she could not, at such short notice, provide her with sleeping accommodation. The room which had been allotted to her before was now occupied. She must kindly make her own arrangements.

Certain though she was that Mrs. Martin would have found room for her, Maura did not argue the matter. She rang up Mrs. Perez who, declaring that she would always be glad to have her at *Mon Abri*, offered her a pleasant first-floor room for the modest rent she had formerly paid for her little attic.

"Geoffrey Fanshawe isn't here any longer, I'm afraid," she told Maura. "He has found a flat in Belleray and will be marrying soon, I gather. That English girl who works at the Florida-Carib. But you know all about that, I expect."

"I didn't. But I'm very pleased." Maura spoke with warm satisfaction "They'll make a very nice couple."

"It's good to hear you say that, my dear. I sometimes thought—! But there's as good fish in the sea—!"

Raymonde's announcement of the news that same afternoon was less good-natured. Clearly annoyed that Maura had found accommodation so quickly and easily, that she would be able to start work at once, she remarked that she was afraid Maura would find it much duller at *Mon Abri* now that her boy-friend had finally defected.

Maura enquired sweetly. "Is he still around?"

"And what about your boy-friend, Dr. Field?"

She felt ashamed next moment for coming down to Raymonde's level of repartee. She had a perfect recollection of Alan Field's recurring anger with Raymonde for her carelessness over his patients. She should have held her tongue.

But Raymonde, though furious, was well able to hold her own.

"The husband I choose won't be an obscure doctor," she retorted scornfully. "Nor shall I go out for my man with a gun."

"Rather a cheap remark, don't you think?" Maura's voice was steady, but she had paled.

Then to her relief the telephone bell rang and Raymonde was obliged to turn away and answer it.

"Oh, yes, Alan!" Maura could have laughed out loud at the change in Raymonde's tone from vinegar to honey. Evidently the "obscure doctor" was still a person to be cultivated—and not only for professional reasons.

"I see!" The honey was a trifle less sweet. "Yes, she's back, as a matter of fact—though you mustn't imagine that she is our only experienced nurse. However, I'll get Sister Baker to speak to you."

To Maura, who was just going out, she said loftily: "Please find Sister Baker as quickly as you can. She'll give you your instructions later."

Shrugging her shoulders over Raymonde's rudeness, Maura went in search of Sister Baker, and found her sitting at a desk in an ante-room, her ball-point poised over the day-book.

"Dr. Field wants you on the telephone," she told her. "Raymonde sent me to fetch you."

"Oh, she did!" was Sister Baker's calm response. "It happens that I have my own desk and own telephone extension now. Couldn't stand that girl fussing round me and giving herself airs, and so I told Mrs. Martin." She took up the receiver, observed coolly: "I'll take the call here, thank you," and a moment later was speaking to Dr. Field, jotting down what he was saying in her notebook.

"A coronary thrombosis? Yes, we can deal with that. Nurse O'Shea? Yes, she'll take on the case. What time are we to expect him?"

Her ball-point went running over the page again, then hanging up the receiver she glanced across at Maura.

"It's Mr. Hewson, the solicitor. One of the most important men in Belleray, as you probably know. Dr. Field wants you to nurse him." She gave a little smile. "He's rather a sweet person, Alan. Said he knew I'd be too busy running things to take on an exacting case. It's true. But he didn't make me feel, as Raymonde tries to, that I'm getting too old to deal with very serious illness."

Maura's Irish temper flared.

"You know ten times more about nursing than she ever will," she said sturdily. "And you're fifty times more likeable! I wish that girl could have a spell of training under Sister Foster, at my old hospital in London." And then she shook her dark head in mock mournfulness. "It wouldn't be any good, though. They wouldn't keep her a week!"

"May I ask who is the object of this interesting if time-wasting conversation?" Raymonde came in quietly from the corridor, and by her expression the two nurses guessed that she had heard most of what they had been saying.

Maura gave her an encouraging grin.

"It's someone we both happen to dislike," she said.

"Or would do, if we felt she was worth that much emotion."

Sister Baker's pleasant brown face took on a greyish tinge—for it seemed, for a second, as though Raymonde would strike Maura.

But two young nursing orderlies came along the corridor just then, and the moment of crisis passed.

Giving Maura a look of pure hatred, Raymonde took her departure.

CHAPTER 9

MAURA, ashamed of losing her temper with Raymonde, was soon trying to put things on a better basis. Open quarrelling in a place dedicated to the care of the sick, a place so small that patients and staff alike would be affected, seemed to her disgraceful. She blushed as she thought of the kind of comment Sister Foster would have made.

Raymonde, however, pampered and ill-disciplined all her life, and furiously jealous of Maura on several counts, preferred to remain on the warpath. She did not, indeed, indulge in overt attacks on her, but she subjected her to innumerable pinpricks which Maura, but for the concentration she was giving to this new case, would have found intolerable.

She would come down to elevenses a few minutes late to find that the iced fruit drinks, so necessary in the tropics, had been cleared quickly away. Essential items of uniform would be unaccountably missing from the laundry-room. A telephone message from Mrs. Gonzalez inviting her to spend a couple of hours with the family on a nearby beach was delayed until it was too late to take advantage of the offer—which had coincided with one of her brief periods of leisure.

Mr. Hewson, the genial and kindly solicitor whom all Belleray liked and respected, proved to be so desperately ill that, but for Sister Baker's insistence, Maura would have taken no time off at all. As it was, nursing him with every ounce of skill and patience that she possessed, she found herself oblivious, not only of Raymonde and her malice, but of all other people, all other matters.

All other people, that is to say, but Paul Lasalle.

There were moments, even when she was on duty, when the sudden thought of him was like a stab-wound. And her scant leisure was clouded with unhappy and restless self-questioning.

She had written to Mrs. Lasalle immediately on her return to Hillside explaining that she was once more sleeping at *Mon Abri* and could be rung there any evening, that she preferred to have any letters sent there. And she had received no reply. Not a line, not a telephone message.

Did this mean the decision to drop her? It seemed odd, considering Mrs. Lasalle's last conversation with her. Had Claude's presence on the island any connection with this strange silence? Were his mother and half-brother waiting to contact her until he and Damaris were safely back in Raballo?

It was Gloria, the night nurse, who gave her a ray of hope.

Taking over from Maura one evening, she remarked bitterly that she would be thankful when Mrs. Martin returned and Raymonde was demoted.

"She had the nerve to comment on the number of times I was writing to my boy-friend," she said indignantly. "Told me in that sarcastic way of hers that I must have plenty of free time to carry on such an extensive correspondence. I'm leaving no more letters in the rack for posting. I put nothing past her!"

"I use the *Mon Abri* address, not Hillside," Maura observed mildly, and then was struck by a sudden recollection.

That letter she had written to Mrs. Lasalle on first coming back to Hillside had been posted from here.

She had slipped it into the rack just as the postman came up the drive. Raymonde would have had to act with great speed to remove it. But it was not an impossibility.

A resolution crystallised in her mind. And the following afternoon she spent what should have been her short rest period in going down by bus to Belleray, getting out at the stop nearest the General Hospital.

Cost her what it might in pride, she was going to ask if she might visit Paul for a few moments. He was certain to be in a private ward, and no difficulties would be made.

But her enquiry at the office in the entrance brought her the news that Paul had left some days earlier and was at home convalescing.

She was turning away, trying to hide her disappointment and murmuring confusedly that she was very glad he was making such a good recovery, when the clerk stopped her.

"Excuse me, miss," he said apologetically, "but aren't you the young lady that was responsible for the unfortunate accident?"

Maura nodded, wondering what was coming, and he went on in a kindly tone: "If you would like the latest report on him, I'll fetch Nurse Rodrigues for you. She's going up to his home every afternoon to give him therapy."

Before Maura could decide whether she wanted to see this Nurse Rodrigues or not, he had turned to the switchboard to make his request.

"She's coming at once," he announced a moment later. "I knew she would. She's that sort." His brown face crinkled in a smile. "No starch about her. Lovely in her looks and lovely in her ways. Best nurse in the hospital, they say—of the younger ones, that is. But of course, new brooms—"

Along came Nurse Rodrigues then—tall, olive skinned, with perfect features and figure, and a wide generous smile, dressed in her outdoor uniform.

"You've arrived just at the right moment," she said. "I'm off to the Lasalle home now. If you'd like to come up and see Paul for yourself, I'll give you a lift."

She couldn't possibly do that, Maura explained. She was nursing a severe coronary, had cut her off-time down to a minimum, and must catch a bus back to Hillside Nursing Home within the next few minutes.

Nurse Rodrigues glanced at her wrist-watch.

"I've just time to run you back there before going to the Lasalles," she said. "We can talk on the way."

"But it's out of your way," Maura demurred.

"Never mind that. You look far too fagged to struggle with buses. Come on now."

In the small hospital car she gave Maura, with typical West Indian frankness, an account not only of Paul's steady progress, but of the rest of the household.

Mrs. Lasalle was pretty tired, she said, but when Maura suggested timidly that this was probably due to her shock over Paul and her subsequent anxiety, she pooh-poohed the idea.

"It's her son Claude and his wife," she said, "and their very badly behaved little boy. They're a hopeless trio to have in a house where there's illness. They went back to Raballo yesterday, thank goodness. Maybe we'll have some peace." And she went on to observe with enthusiasm that Mrs. Lasalle was "a sweetie." As for Paul, he was a real charmer, though given to bouts of depression at times.

"It must have been frightful for you, finding you'd shot him," she said sympathetically. "But the Lasalles don't bear you a bit of ill-will. Except for Damaris, Claude's wife. She was a bit catty about you—which was silly, considering she's never met you. Not a bad kid, though."

And then, having finished discussing the Lasalle family, she turned her attention to Maura herself, asking why she didn't come to work at the hospital, where conditions had improved greatly of late, and would certainly compare well with those at a small nursing home.

"I'm not staying on in the Caribbean," Maura explained. "I'm either going home to Ireland, via England, or else trying my luck in South America." And she told Nurse Rodrigues of her friendship with the Gonzalez family, of their suggestion that she would easily find a good post nursing in the Argentine.

"I bet you would, with your training. I've heard all about you—or quite a lot, anyway. Incidentally, I'm pretty well trained myself. The new hospital at Raballo can stand comparison with quite a few hospitals in England and the States, so I'm told."

Maura forbore to tell her that she had nearly gone there with her friend, Gwen Davies, from London: it might have involved awkward explanations in regard to her decision to turn down the idea. Nor did she nerve herself to ask from whom her companion had learnt so much about her.

In any case further conversation was impossible, for they had reached the open gate of Hillside, where

Nurse Rodrigues deposited her and bade her a cheery good-bye.

Maura didn't feel quite so cheerful! This Nurse Rodrigues was not only lovely to look at, but full of vitality and charm. And she was seeing Paul constantly. Here, maybe, was the reason for his silence.

But she was smiling when she went back to her patient, and his face, too, lit up at the sight of her.

"I'm getting terribly possessive, Nurse," he said. "My wife's been here this afternoon and she's been scolding me for fretting when you're not around. As far as she's capable of scolding, that is."

Maura straightened his sheet.

"You've not been neglected, I'm sure, Mr. Hewson," she said, with gentle reproach. "Sister Baker promised to keep an eye on you."

"And so she has. She's a great little woman. But she hasn't that soft Irish voice of yours, Nurse O'Shea."

She laughed.

" 'Tis yourself is the blarneying Irish fellow," she told him.

"My clients say I'm a bit on the dour side, so I hear!" And then he gestured towards a great basket of luscious tropical fruit. "My wife says I'm to share this with you, so you'd better take some away to that *pension* of yours before Miss Raymonde interferes. Incidentally, my wife sent you her usual message—a regular theme song, it's becoming—that she can never express her gratitude for your care of me. You and that night-nurse, she says, are a couple of angels. And I thoroughly agree. When I'm well, we're going to take you both for a spree."

Maura gave him a swift, professional glance.

"You're looking better to-day," she said. "Maybe

the spree will come off sooner than we could have hoped. But you're talking too much. I'll hump up your pillows and you must try to relax. You've an hour before your next injection."

To Maura's deep satisfaction this slow improvement continued, and she had the wonderful feeling that, through the faith of his many friends, she was being allowed to bring back this greatly loved man from the brink of the grave. Certainly she was doing everything in her power in a practical way to foster his recovery, and the strain of it was showing on her face. She was beginning to look very tired indeed.

So much so that on the eve of her next day off Sister Baker insisted that an odd hour or two of free time was not enough—that she must take the whole day.

She was too proud to ring up the Lasalles, as she would have loved to do. Even if Mrs. Lasalle had not received that letter she had left to be posted at Hillside, she and Paul would know now that she had been to the hospital to enquire after Paul. Nurse Rodrigues would certainly have told them.

She must resign herself to the dismal fact that the Lasalles had no wish to keep in touch with her for some reason best known to themselves.

Instead she telephoned to Mrs. Gonzalez, and received a cordial invitation to come at once and stay as long as she could. Rita, her sister-in-law, would drive over to fetch her directly after breakfast, and in due course she arrived at *Mon Abri* accompanied by her excited little niece.

Rita's warm manner, and young Stella's hugs and kisses, brought a surface healing to Maura's hurt. There was something after all in that old tag about counting your blessings. Here she was travelling in congenial company through what must surely be one of the most beautiful islands in the world—an island which thousands of people spending monotonous lives in grim, grey cities would give anything to visit, which frustrated, hard-up artists would long to paint.

She made a conscious effort to impress on her mind the details of this drive through a countryside of tree-covered mountains and green valleys on a switchback road from which every now and then, one caught glimpses of a sapphire sea, streaked with jade. A countryside ceilinged by a cobalt sky, flecked inevitably by a cloud or two, pearly and light as a feather from a dove's breast. She must remember the brilliant flowering trees, the bright-plumaged tropical birds with their strange cries, the little villages of tiny wooden houses, set in plots planted with bananas and cassava, where people waved a greeting, their brown faces smiling.

All this, and so much more, must be imprinted in her memory—for maybe within a few weeks she would have left the Caribbean for ever, never to return.

Mrs. Gonzalez was delighted to see her, and after a delicious lunch, Stella having been sent off for a nap, she and Rita settled down in comfortable chairs on the veranda for coffee and a chat.

Maura had noticed at once that Mrs. Gonzalez was still pale, with dark shadows under her beautiful eyes. It had surprised her a little, for she had read in the paper, a few days earlier, that there was to be no trial of Manoel after all. He had been found insane by the leading doctors of the place, and, there being no mental hospital in the island in which a psychopath could safely be held, he was being taken under strong escort to a large, modern institution in Raballo.

"It must be an enormous relief to you not having to go to court and give evidence," she remarked to her.

Mrs. Gonzalez nodded.

"I've been dreading it more than I can say. Not only the actual ordeal in court, but the stirring up of terrible memories which I've been trying so hard to forget."

"Now you really will forget them," Maura said with quick sympathy. But Mrs. Gonzalez shook her head wearily, and Rita broke in: "She says, poor darling, that she'll never escape from the horror of that night so long as she lives in this house."

"Nor so long as I stay in Ste. Monique," Mrs. Gonzalez added, with an uncontrollable shudder.

"But the same sort of thing might conceivably happen anywhere," Maura pointed out, and reminded them of the attack which had been made on her in a crowded London street, and about which she had already spoken to them.

"I know all that," Mrs. Gonzalez agreed wearily, "but reasoning doesn't help. I'm certain that Stella and I ought to be out of the islands altogether, for a year or two at least, perhaps for ever, and Carlos, who is so sweet and understanding, has agreed. As soon as he can find a reliable manager for his interests here—within a couple of months, he hopes—he is going to sell this house and take us home to the Argentine."

"I shall miss you all badly." And indeed Maura felt genuinely sad at the thought of never seeing this kindly family again, of losing all contact with Stella. "But probably I'll be leaving the Caribbean before you. I've put my name down for a flight to England. And though it's not at all that easy to get a seat at this time of year, I'm expecting an offer any day now."

"Why not put off your return to Europe for a year or two, and come to South America with us?" It was not the first time that one or other member of the Gonzalez family had made this suggestion, but now it was clear that Mrs. Gonzalez was speaking in earnest. "You want to take every chance of seeing the world while you're young, and Fate may never bring you this way again. Besides," she added with a little smile that chased the shadows from her face, "there are a great many eligible bachelors in the Argentine —and Irish girls are very popular with them."

Maura did her best to give a suitably amused smile, but Rita, leaning forward, remarked with a gentleness unusual to her: "You don't seem very happy, Maura. Are things all right at the nursing home? Is this heart case too much for you?"

"Oh, it's not that. Not at all!" Maura's reply came quickly, and with conviction. "I couldn't be keener on nursing. And though I've had anxious moments over this particular patient, he's making a marvellous recovery." And then, the light going out of her face again, she said wearily: "I've had some pretty trying personal problems since I came out here. I think I'll feel better when I've definitely decided what to do and where to go."

"You certainly will," Mrs. Gonzalez told her earnestly. "I'm beginning to relax, now we've fixed to go back home. Maybe if you could make up your mind to come to the Argentine with us, and nurse out there, this tension you're suffering from would snap."

Maura took a deep breath.

"I'll think it over seriously," she said, "and let you

know within a week. And whether I come or not I'll never forget your kindness."

And she thought: "A week—I'll know by then for sure whether there's any hope for me, any chance that Paul will ever come to care." But in her heart of hearts she felt miserably certain that there was no hope for her at all.

Carlos arrived home for dinner, and afterwards volunteered to drive her home. Ordinarily she would have gone straight back to the *pension*, but halfway there she began to have the strangest feeling that she ought to call in first at the nursing home. And though Carlos tried in a big-brotherly way to dissuade her, telling her that it was sheer nerves, he agreed to drop her there for a few minutes, and then take her on to *Mon Abri*.

When she reached the nursing home it was all she could do to control her growing panic, to walk sedately up the path, instead of running. Something was wrong. She was as sure of it as though she had received an alarming telephone message from the home, before leaving the Gonzalez house.

And a moment later she found that she was right.

Alan Field was in the little hall with Raymonde and Sister Baker, and as he caught sight of her his anxious face relaxed.

"Thank God you've come," he cried. "Hewson's taken a turn for the worse. Can you possibly stay for a few hours? Gloria's doing her best, but he shouldn't be left."

"This is quite unnecessary," Raymonde put in sharply. "I'll look after Mr. Hewson myself, if Gloria just puts me wise to his needs."

But Alan shook his head.

"You'd do your best," he said shortly, "but you

haven't the experience. Give Maura a shake-down in the patient's room, so that she'll at least get some physical rest."

"Sorry, but I can't do that," Raymonde began, but Sister Baker intervened.

"I'm in charge of the nursing side, Dr. Field," she said quietly. "Just leave it to me to carry out your instructions."

"That's fine, Sister Baker." And then he looked at Maura. "If there is a still worse development, ring me up at once," and off he went, leaving the three women standing there.

"A lot of hooey!" It was Raymonde who spoke. "As if you were indispensable, Maura! Incidentally, there was a telephone message for you. One of the orderlies took it and wrote it down. But I can't look for it now. It must wait until to-morrow."

Without giving Maura a chance to protest, she disappeared in the direction of her room.

"Don't worry," Sister Baker murmured. "I'll have a look in the office and if I can find it you shall have it."

Maura thanked her, and went out to tell Carlos what had happened, and with the sudden hope that the message might be from Paul fairly flew back into the hall. But Sister Baker had no luck, and Maura, switching her mind on to her patient, went off, just as she was in search of Gloria.

And Gloria exclaimed, just as Dr. Field had done: "Thank God you've come!"

CHAPTER 10

MAURA was never, so long as she lived, to forget that anxious night.

On Sister Baker's orders she brought Mrs. Martin's own lightweight garden chair into the sickroom, so that she could keep her feet up and avoid swollen ankles—a common trouble in the tropics, even among younger people, when normal rest is denied.

But she spent little time in that chair.

Mr. Hewson, though semi-conscious, was all too evidently in great pain. And though she could do little for him beyond administering at the correct time the drug which Dr. Field had left for him, she was alert to every change of pulse, of colour, ready on the instant to give him sips of cool fruit-juice when he showed the least sign of thirst, to help him shift his posture when discomfort was added to pain, to alter the air-conditioning in the early hours, when the temperature of the room became too low for him.

At five o'clock, when the Angelus rang out and the cocks and dogs of the neighbourhood began their clamour, Sister Baker slipped in, and beckoned her to come out into the corridor.

"I want you to go up to my room and get a nap," she told Maura quietly. "I'll take on Mr. Hewson. You'll be called in time to join me on day duty at eight o'clock." And then she added: "I've put fresh linen on the bed and a clean nightdress handy, so you can doss down right away. Even a couple of hours' sleep will help you."

Maura obeyed her thankfully, and within minutes was sleeping heavily in Sister Baker's room.

She could have gone on until midday, but at twenty past seven a young auxiliary brought her coffee and fruit and crisp rolls, and a few minutes before eight, fed, bathed and dressed, she was ready to go on duty.

Coming out into the corridor, she ran straight into Raymonde who, stopping her, asked her icily what she was doing in Sister Baker's room.

"Sleeping," Maura returned laconically. "Sister Baker sent me off duty at five o'clock."

"Sister Baker seems to be getting a little above herself. From what I heard last night I understood that Dr. Field was expecting you to spend the whole night with your patient." She paused, then asked: "Can I take it that Mr. Hewson's condition has improved—noticeably, I mean?"

"It hadn't, when I left him." Maura determined to keep her temper, to refrain from reminding Raymonde that Sister Baker was in charge of the nursing arrangements. "I'm going now to take over." And then she observed steadily: "You said last night that there was a telephone message for me. May I have it, please?"

"Of course." Raymonde fumbled in the pocket of her overall. Then, handing a folded slip of paper to Maura, she said: "It's good news. The travel agents have secured a seat for you on the plane leaving for Europe on Thursday. I took the liberty of accepting in your name, and said that you'd confirm it."

Maura stared at her aghast.

"But that's in two days' time. I can't leave Mr. Hewson like that."

"My dear girl, it's about time you learned that no one is indispensable. My aunt is sending us another nurse whom she's come across while away. She arrives by air on Friday."

"But this is tantamount to sending me away without notice!" Maura exclaimed. "In the middle of a case."

"Nonsense. You've made it clear for long enough that you were most unsettled here."

And now Maura made the blunt observation that so far she had been holding back.

"You are not in charge of the nursing side here. It's for Sister Baker to decide. And I know very well what her decision will be."

And with that she walked away.

Mr. Hewson was still desperately ill and Sister Baker, handing over, told her that at his wife's urgent request, his old friend the Bishop would be coming in an hour's time to give him the Last Sacraments.

Busy as she was, attending to her patient, and getting the room ready for the Bishop's visit, Maura thrust all other matters out of her mind—the sharp disappointment that the telephone message had not come from Paul, the idea that Raymonde was trying to force her out of the island at this disgracefully short notice. Time enough for considering all this later on, when she had a chance of talking to Sister Baker.

Mrs. Hewson arrived in due course—deeply anxious, but too courageous to show grief. Her husband was conscious now, and free at the moment from great pain, and his poor, weary face lightened when he heard that the Bishop was on his way.

Silver-haired and fatherly, with an expression of deep kindliness, the Bishop, in his white cotton cassock, brought a sense of peace, a relief from tension, into the little room. Quietly he performed the rites for the healing of the sick, and when Communion had been given to the patient, and the last pleading prayer for his recovery said, he came out into the corridor with Mrs. Hewson, and Maura heard him say, putting his hand on her shoulder: "I am sure God is not calling him yet. But we must go on praying—praying hard."

During the rest of that day there was no evident change in the sick man's condition, and it was with difficulty that Maura found time for that urgent conversation with Sister Baker.

As she expected, Sister was highly indignant over what she termed Raymonde's preposterous behaviour.

She knew already that Mrs. Martin had managed to find another good nurse, over in St. Jacques, but this had nothing to do with the emergency over Mr. Hewson. Even had Maura been staying on indefinitely another experienced nurse was essential at Hillside.

"And Raymonde is in no position to tell you to leave," she declared. "Even if she was, you're entitled to proper notice. The trouble is that she's eaten up with jealousy of you, and won't be happy until you're out of the Caribbean. But don't worry. Ring up the Travel agency and say you won't be wanting that seat. There's absolutely nothing she can do."

Dr. Field, bringing the good news that he had secured the services of a temporary nurse to look after Mr. Hewson at night, was very angry when he learned, through Sister Baker, of Raymonde's efforts to send Maura away forthwith. He agreed that "all this nonsense" must be ignored. Raymonde would then pipe down. For, with Sister Baker in charge, there was really nothing she could do.

However, the very next day showed that this optimism was ill-founded. An official letter arrived for Maura demanding her attendance at the Labour Office, it having been reported to them that she had landed on the island under false pretences and was undertaking paid work without a labour permit. They would expect her to call at the Town Hall in the course of the morning.

Sister Baker rang up immediately, explaining that Maura was nursing Mr. Hewson, who was very seriously ill. Could the officials possibly excuse her from coming to see them until she had finished with this case?

But the reply she received was adamant in its refusal.

Miss O'Shea had been nursing for months in the island without a permit and, moreover, had lied about her reason for coming to Ste. Monique. She should really have been tackled before, when there was all that publicity about her in the papers. It had been sheer oversight. Unless she could provide a satisfactory answer, she would be requested to leave on a plane for Europe almost immediately.

Schedules had quickly to be altered, and Maura, pale with distress and worry, caught the first possible bus down to Belleray.

By sheer bad luck, the officer normally in charge of the Labour Office was away on holiday, and the young man acting for him was determined to carry out the regulations to the letter—and even beyond it, if it seemed well to him.

He pointed out that Maura, on landing, had signed a paper to say that she had come to Ste. Monique to marry one Mr. Lasalle. Instead she had at once, so his information went, started a paid job, nursing at the Hillside Home. He wanted no explanations—merely the facts.

The form, giving her reason for landing, he already had, duly signed by her. Would she now say whether or not she had been engaged in paid work almost since the day of her arrival in the island?

She tried to explain, despite his ban on anything but a plain "yes" or "no" to his questions, and was conscious of sympathetic glances from two other clerks, working at desks at the other side of the room. But he was adamant.

"If people from this island slip into England on a false declaration, and take paid work without a permit, they are promptly sent home. Why should you expect different treatment here?"

One of the other clerks made an effort then to intervene.

"Mr. Garcia," he remarked apologetically, "I think if Mr. Pereira had been here, and not on holiday, he wouldn't have been so severe. The very fact that she is nursing Mr. Hewson—and the strong likelihood that she had no intention of deceiving—"

"I'm sorry, but I must conform with the regulations." Mr. Garcia's tone was sharply hostile. "Miss O'Shea, I have ascertained that there is a vacant seat on the plane leaving for Europe to-morrow. You will be required to travel on this plane—the consequences of your failing to do so being serious."

Stunned, Maura made her way to the door, and the second of the other clerks hurried to open it for her.

"It didn't help, your nursing Mr. Hewson," he murmured, as he ushered her out. "Mr. Garcia lost a law-suit through Mr. Hewson intervening on the other side. I only wish Mr. Pereira were here. He'd have treated you differently, I know."

And then, on the pretence of guiding her to the bus stop, he added: "It's the lady in charge of Hillside Nursing Home who's at the bottom of all this trouble. My, miss, she must be your enemy! Sending us old newspaper cuttings to call our attention to you."

His kind brown face was troubled, and Maura managed to thank him for his consideration. The next instant he had slipped back into the office, and Maura was alone on the busy street.

Her legs were trembling under her, and because she felt the absolute necessity of sitting down for a moment she crossed the road, threading her way through the traffic, and went into the lounge of the Florida-Carib. A few minutes' rest, and an ice-cold drink, and she would be ready to go back to Hillside and tell Sister Baker what had happened.

The first person she saw was Phyllis, hurrying along with the lunch menus. She stopped at once when she caught sight of Maura and, shocked at her appearance, told her to go along to her room, where she would join her immediately.

Too near collapse to argue that she had not enough time, that she must rush back to her patient, she did as she was told. And almost at once Phyllis reappeared with a tray of iced pineapple juice.

"What on earth is the matter, Maura?" she demanded, handing her a tall glass. "You look positively ill."

"I'm just about at the end of my tether," Maura returned desperately. And with Phyllis's encouragement she was soon blurting out, utterly thankful to have someone in whom she could confide, the whole story of the misery and anxiety which had been haunting her, its culmination in what was practically deportation.

Phyllis, happy in her plans for marriage with Geoffrey, had lost every trace of hostility towards Maura. She had forgotten her former jealousy, and remembered that it was to this broken-looking girl that she owed her life.

So kind she was, so sympathetic, that Maura kept back nothing. It all came out like a torrent—even her love for Paul and her agony of mind over its hopelessness—the bitter prospect that after to-morrow she would probably never set eyes on him again.

At that, Phyllis sat up with a jerk.

"But you haven't been very friendly to him and his mother," she remarked. "Not even polite! When they rang up to know if you could give Paul therapy in the afternoons you sent, so Paul told me, a very curt message: that you were deeply involved in serious nursing, and couldn't possibly break up your time like that. And that in any case you were shortly leaving Ste. Monique for South America, with the Gonzalez family."

Maura stared at her blankly, her face whiter than ever.

"I received no message, and sent none," she said. "This must be more of Raymonde's trickery. But it's too late to do anything now. It's not as though Paul had ever cared for me—the way I care for him." Her voice broke, as she added: "You might tell him some time that I—I wasn't really discourteous to him and his mother."

Then pulling herself together with a great effort, she glanced at her watch. "I must get back to Hillside," she said. "Ring me a taxi, dear. I can't neglect my patient to-day because of what is going to happen to-morrow."

The first person she ran into, on reaching Hillside, was Raymonde, setting an imposing flower arrangement in the entrance hall.

"Well?" she enquired airily, "how did you get on?"

"As you've probably been enquiring already on the telephone, you'll be aware that I'm ordered to leave Ste. Monique to-morrow by plane." Maura spoke with the greatest bitterness. "You call yourself a nurse—and jeopardise the life of a patient!"

"Are you insinuating that I've had anything to do with your sudden repatriation?" Raymonde's defiance did not ring true—she could not meet Maura's eyes.

"*Insinuating*! I'm stating that you've done all this deliberately—out of sheer hatred."

"Theatrical nonsense! Actually, if you hadn't been so keen on dramatising yourself—posing as having saved the Reeves girl's life from drowning, peppering Paul Lasalle with a shotgun—you wouldn't have been noticed by the labour officials."

"There's only one word with which to describe you," Maura told her icily. "I give you three guesses." And with that she hurried off to change and take on the care of her patient.

She found a moment to tell Sister Baker that she was being forced to leave next day, and hadn't known until then how angry that small brown woman could be. As for Alan Field, any hopes that Raymonde might have cherished in regard to him, contemptuous denials notwithstanding, were killed for all time.

Both pressed her to take the rest of the day off to make her preparations, insisting that somehow or other Mr. Hewson would be looked after, but Maura refused. She would find time during the evening and next morning: the plane did not leave until the afternoon.

Mr. Hewson, just about holding his own, achieved a faint smile as she bent over him to give him his midday dose of medicine, and murmured that he had been missing her all morning.

"I must be getting into my second childhood," he whispered, bringing out each word with difficulty. "I fret for you, like a baby for its mother."

In different circumstances Maura would have been highly amused at the idea of "mothering" this grey-haired sixty-year-old, but now his words sharply increased her pain and misery.

If only Mrs. Martin had been here, Raymonde could never have carried out a plan which must inevitably cause a setback to a patient's recovery—if it did not, at this time of crisis, endanger his life. It was an especially wicked course of conduct when there was such a shortage of trained nurses at Hillside.

When she went to have her lunch—a scrambled affair these days—Raymonde was speaking on the telephone, and seeing Maura she beckoned to her.

"It's Paul Lasalle, ringing up to say good-bye to you," she remarked, and passed on, a triumphant little smile on her face. "He's off to St. Jacques to-night, he says."

But Paul did not, it seemed, mean to make his good-byes over the telephone.

"I'll be up in fifteen minutes, Maura," he said, in answer to her shaky, "Hullo!" He went on quickly: "Raymonde says you'll be on duty again by then, but I must see you. I leave for St. Jacques at four o'clock, and shan't be back for three days."

"Very well." She hung up the receiver, with the tears trickling down her face. At least he was coming to say good-bye in person. That would be a small, precious memory to cherish in the years ahead. It showed that he wasn't altogether indifferent.

She ate her lunch—toyed with it, rather—with her eyes wandering continually to the clock. Ten minutes later she heard the low hoot of his horn.

"Excuse me, Raymonde," she said hastily, and was out of the dining-room in an instant, and through the front door. Every moment counted now. She had so painfully few to spare.

He was standing by his car, looking very pale and tense, and motioned to her to get in.

"I can't go for a drive, or anything like that," she told him quickly. "Can't leave Mr. Hewson for more than a few minutes."

"I prefer to talk in the car," he returned brusquely. "If I stepped inside that house I might be tempted to wring Raymonde's neck! Quick, now!"

She got in hastily, in far too chaotic a condition of mind to resent his curtness, and he said at once: "I've been talking to Phyllis Reeves. She rang me up at the office, and I went straight along to see her. I gather you forgot to get a labour permit, and that Raymonde has gone behind your back and created a stink."

Maura nodded. "It's horrible of her—especially when I'm nursing a coronary thrombosis, and there's no really efficient nurse to take my place."

"Beastly as I've been to you—a jealous beast at that—I always said you were a fine nurse. It's natural you should feel so badly about having to leave your patient. But, Maura," and his arm went round her, "is there any other reason why it distresses you to leave Ste. Monique like this?"

She was crying openly as she looked up at him.

"What has Phyllis been saying to you?" she stammered.

"Enough to make me realise that Raymonde is an adept at suppressing letters and telephone calls when she's indulging one of her hates. But that's a minor issue, considering the few minutes we have left. I've been horrible to you, I know. And Phyllis has told me something else! That I'm a blind fool not to grasp that you felt for me just what I felt about you—that you love me, Maura!"

"And now it's too late," she sobbed, her face in her hands. "Once they repatriate a person, as they call it, they never let them come back. At least that's what I've heard."

"My dear, I'm going to see that you stay on this island as long as you wish—permanently, I hope. You see, one of the grievances they have against you in the Labour Office is that you signed a declaration that you were marrying a man named Lasalle."

"I know—but when I tried to explain—"

"Leave me to do that, my sweet," he said. "All I want is your consent to marry a different member of the Lasalle family. To marry me. I've just time to see about a special licence, and arrange our marriage for the very day I get back from Ste. Monique.

"But your mother?" she faltered.

He gave her an odd look.

"She's always liked you—a lot," he said. "But it's true she was doubtful about the wisdom of our marrying. That's Claude's fault. The silly fellow still sentimentalises over you behind his wife's back—and that made her nervous. However," and he scowled, "if I can't protect my wife from the languishing glances and sights of a stupid and grotesquely weak brother—"

"You wouldn't have to," she exclaimed. "Oh, Paul, are you sure you can get that licence?"

"Certain! I made enquiries before I rang you up."

"And you won't mind my finishing out this case?" She had suddenly remembered Mr. Hewson, and her solicitude for him came flooding back.

"Of course. I've no objection to your carrying on with *day* nursing until he's better."

She coloured.

"I'm sure he's going to get well," she told him. "There couldn't be a black cloud on all this happiness. The Bishop himself said so—and he's a pretty wise sort of person."

"That reminds me. He'll marry us in his own private chapel. He christened me, you know. How would that suit you?"

She smiled, though her cheeks were still wet.

"The most junior curate would do," she said. "It's the bridegroom that matters."

And then she glanced at her watch.

"I must fly," she exclaimed. "This minute!"

"No, the next," he quipped. "There's just time for this." And gathering her up in his arms, he kissed her reddened eyes, her wet cheeks, and then with an impetuosity which roused in her a joyous response, her soft yielding lips.